The
WORDSMITHS
at GORSEMERE

SUE LIMB

BANTAM PRESS

NEW YORK · LONDON · TORONTO · SYDNEY · AUCKLAND

March 14th 1799

Day. of V.V.Great Joy!! For today we removed to
Vole Cottage, in Cumberland. A _dear_ place!
Not quite _in_ the village (of Gorsemere), & not quite
out! But nestling under the majestic peaks, of
Flabbergoat Fell! So fatigued can scarce hold
my. pen. Worn out with carrying cupboards, etc.
up the steep bank to the house.

W^m asleep on the sopha. I have placed a bunch
of Toadflax by his head. So v. weary can scar

Toad-Flax
(quite
rampant)
by the Sod-
Wall!)

March 18th. So fatigued last night,
fell asleep at my journal! And this ——→
dozing stream of ink, is the result. W^m says,
it looks like the course of the River Pudden,
a local torrent. The darling! (W^m, I mean)
This shows so clearly, the penetrating power of his
Fancy! A line of ink, transfigured into a
mountain Beck! It reminds me, that when I have
leisure, I intend to _dangle_ my toes in the Pudden!

Unpacked, etc. No sign of the teapot.
Am obliged to make tea, in an -other Vessel, ~~and~~
~~am not sure if it is altogether~~ Rained, incessantly.

March 19th

A lovely day – much warmer rain. Still unloading carts, but no sign of the teapot, alas. I am worn out with carrying wardrobes & beds upstairs, though ably assisted by William, who sat upon the landing, the better to direct my efforts. We were watched by a dear Cumberland cow, thro' the window.

After dinner, whilst I was tossing the slops upon the Horsetail, I spied a red-headed fellow lurking in a Hazel-hedge nearby. He was busy with a note-book and pencil and seemed to be observing me closely. W^m was resting indoors (he had been working upon a short lyric, _The Sod Wall_ & had overtaxed his imagination) so I sprang into the hazel bush, and challenged the fellow, as to his purpose?

– Dear Madam – he said – Heaven forbid that I should disturb you. I am an artist in pen & in oils: my name, is Samuel PICKERELL –

– Mr William Brake – he cried – is my Spirituall Mentor: he converses with ANGELS, Madam – I express^d surprise!

Alas I cannot execute cows! W^m says, it reminds him of his old Latin-master, who had a _lolling_ tongue!

Hair v. disarrayed still he is an Artist!

Profile, of Mr Pickerell! Not a great beauty!

Poor Mr P, at Home!!

— I dogged Mr Brake's footsteps day & night, — continued Mr Pickerell — desirous to learn of him, all of his art, until he was so kind as to suggest, my skills might benefit from a long trip to the Far North......

'Twas my plan — sighed Mr Pickerell — to execute some LITHOGRAPHS of THISTLETHWAITE —

.... At this moment, Mr Pickerell was so unfortunate, as to spit directly into my eye! I stood blinking for quite five minutes. Poor P. mortified, gazed at the sod wall & quite lost his drift.

Poor Mr Pickerell! He had spent all his money on paper and pens, and was at present living in a hollow oak nearby. I offered him the sanctuary of our wash-house, but begged him always to sketch quietly, so as not to distract my dear William from his work. — For, I confided, — this must remain the most profound secret, Mr P. — but I must tell you that my brother William is a very great poet! Perhaps the greatest poet in all England !!!

Italian
Reading
List !!:

Dante
Petrarcha
Bruni
Niccolò Niccoli
Dapiccoli
Savanarola
Luni
Vespucci
Ugociccioli

(Goodness!
It rhymes!
My first
canzone!)

At this news, Mr P. was overjoyed, & offered at once
to execute William's likeness. I gave Mr P.
permission to follow us about at a discreet
distance, & sketch us at our daily tasks. I will
make a few pages of this little book available
to him, as he is a fellow-artist in adversity.

Mr P. spied the sketch I had made, of the
Cow, & said it had quite the CINQUECENTO
CHIAROSCURO. — Not sure what this means
(must revive my Italian!) but think it must
be a disease of cattle. Indeed, now I recall,
I am sure my Great Aunt Judith had a
CHIAROSCURO just below her GOITRE, & it
used to ache in the rain

NB Have
found the
Teapot !!

Dante - The Divine
and strangely, I feel
he resembles — Dear William
somewhat!

My own humble sketches
— Not Mr P's !

March 20th

Scrubbed the floors, & beat the rag-rugs against the hawthorn tree, in the lane.

Wrote to —

Dear Cholericke — inviting him to stay

Mary Hitchinson — thanking her for cloves, etc

The Publisher John Macmurray — sent him copies of Wms latest works. Perhaps… who knows….?

Hannah More — praising her inspiring pamphlet !!

Josiah Wedgwood — asking for a loan, of 200£

The dreadful Pitt — protesting against the recent repressive legislation.

Aunt Alice — asking her to send on my nether—garments, which I have unaccountably left behind at Keighley! William, wrote to the poet Percy Jelley.

Alas! a poor EARWIG had the misfortune, to be caught between the pages of my journal!

To Soda 6d

To Oysters 2½d

To Starch 3d

To Beeswax . . . . . . ¾d

To Ink . . £2 -10s -3d

Very windy today. Felt it very much.

March 21st— A letter from my dear friend Mary Hitchinson, who sent a book of the classification of BIRDS. I turn its pages with great joy, and when domestic dut̲_____

March 22nd— Wm called for his tea, then! I had been lost in clouds of Bearded Tits! This day vanished in a welter of scrubbing, hammering, etc from which William fled up to Chattering Crags & brought me back a sweet stone.

March 23rd— So v. tired, could only dig the garden for 6 hours. Wm kindly helped, by carrying out the seed-packets. Only an inch of top soil: We are in dire need of DUNG.

March 24th— Slept late — rouz̲d̲ up by Wm complaining, that there was only porridge to be had. Mortified at my bad housekeeping. Feel sure a TWITE is nesting in the Necessary! ~So glad!!

Tomorrow we will venture forth in search of dung, and provisions, with Mr P. in attendance. As to his art: I feel his line is fine, but I wish he would wash more often.

For colds: Infusion of Lungwort Plantain & Coltsfood: Apply with damp sponge, to the navel.

Twite's Egg
not to
be confused
with

Whimbrel's !
- Easily
Done !

March 26th

    William, distressed by the incessant CHWEEK CHWEEK of the TWITE, has removed its nest from the Necessary House, to an old apple tree, in the orchard. He often composes in the Privy. So unfortunate, it should disturb him! - I am sorry, Dorothy - he said (considerate as ever!) - but I am endeavouring, to rewrite _The Sod Wall_, & the Bird - Noise wracks my nerves — V. anxious for my dear Brother's nerves. Anxious also for the Twite's eggs.

March 27th

    William smiled today!! I am so glad he feels content in our new home! Vole cottage peeps out shyly from a steep bank, with a kitchen garden beyond, where today I sowed Lovage, Borage, Cabbage, Beaked Saxifrage, & Shaggy Persiflage. ~~The orchard above, is a blessed~~ ~~haven~~ ~~spot~~, & the grey ~~mists of Gossemere~~ spread out ~~all around, bring to this devine~~ ~~spot~~ retreat such an air ~~of~~ heavenly ~~peace, my heart seems~~ ~~to hum~~ sing ~~with contentment.~~ "This Demi Paradise" ~~as~~ ~~Milton~~ Shakespeare (- was it?) ~~described dear~~ ~~England. Oh Dear!~~

My powers
of Expression
~~removed~~
Deserted
me !

O the darling! He has used a page of my humble Journal, to perfect his <u>Sod-Wall</u>!

~~The Wall of Sods~~
The Sod-Wall

six
bix
sticks
kicks
~~ticks~~
licks
nicks
micks
ticks
vicks
wicks
dicks
flicks

thumb
bumb
crumb
dumb
numb
plub

sods
bods
cods
gods
pods

Of modest height, some two foot six
~~It runs along the front of~~ It skirts about our cot
Of modest earth, heaved up in bricks
I'd tell you if 'twas not.
I sat upon it morn & eve
~~To pick my nose and stare~~ To contemplate the lane
~~I had one of my migraines~~ My head did ache, my heart did heave
~~The weather was appalling~~ Beneath the hail and rain.
I thought of one long gone before
~~A rather puny child~~ Some three foot two: not tall
I hear her merry voice no more
~~Her name was Edwina Jemima Huddlestone~~ Her name I can't recall.
I asked her age, that sweet wild rose
With laugh so mad and gay
~~Then to her nose she raised~~ She raised her thumb up to her nose
And laughed, & ran away.
And now I sit and think and rhyme
Upon this same sod-wall
From break of day to dinner-time
And never stir at all.

W.W., 1799

And here are some of his <u>dear</u> <u>doodles</u> !!

Strange... I do not seem able to recollect an Emotion
What a wondrous thing is the masculine Organ of Speculation!
O Heav'n! I have forgot to write to Sara!
SP

The Orchard

March 28th

The Twite has left its nest: its eggs are cold.
Sobbed for an hour upon the orchard grass.
William began a lyric: The Emigrant Twite,
but I think it will not do.

Dear
Vole Cottage!

March 29th

Have just come in from a walk to Nattering
Bottoms, to find some letters: one from poor
Cholericke (bad in his bowels again, alas!)
He is a letter from dear Mary, who tells of a
famous strong man of Yorkshire, one Willie
Farley, who runs up mountains with bricks
tied to his head, to increase the difficulty. —
Oh ——

Provisions
needed
Nutmeg
Suet
Gelatine
Cochineal
Juniper
berries
Ox cheeks
tapioca
Rooks
Agar-agar

March 30th

Was forced to break off my journal there,
as Wm fainted! And lay insensible, for many
minutes!! It was provoked by his receiving a
copy of a new satirical poem by Lord Byro - the
most disgraceful attack upon poor Wm's work!
Ignorant, vulgar and full of indecent innuendo!!

W^m has been confined to his bed ever since. He eats heartily, thank G—! But his groans are terrible to hear & his water is quite _purple_! The Dame's Tonsils are out.

April 1st Distinctly heard the Kikki-kirrick of the Pratincole in the orchard this morning. And then a letter from London, from the publisher John Macmurray, offering to publish some of W^{m's} poems! W^m leapt from his bed, seized a piece of cheese, and strode off up the Devil's Danglers whistling Lillibolero! So glad.

    In his absence, I cleaned W^{m's} room: polish'd the books, sharpened the pens, etc. Then I starched three of his shirts, mended the curtain where he had torn it in rage at Lord Byro, and darned the seat of W^{m's} woollen nether–stocks, which had worn quite through upon (as it were) the Seat of Learning. (V. much diverted by this thought !!! Tho. William appeared too ~~sunk in thought~~ contemplative upon his return, to absorb my meaning.)

Dame's
Tonsils
(a Cumberland
Orchid! –)
Amygdalae
Matronalis

To _Soften_
Flannel:
Thrash it, under
clear running
water, with
a petrified
pig's leg.

April 3rd

Our next neighbour, Mrs Grindstone, an ancient dame, who lives in a mossy cottage, beyond the bend in the lane, was kind enough to send us a Cockerell, brought by a little ragged boy. The boy ~~dost~~ told me, that the Cockerell had killed a mountain-goat, by pecking out its brains! I wished Mrs Grindstone had wrung its neck, before presenting us with it. No sooner had the boy gone, than the bird escaped its wicker cage, ~~pecked~~ gave my ankle a vicious peck, & flew up to the roof of the Necessary, where it set up the most insolent trumpeting!!

April 4th A lovely day. A migrant SCAUP (I recognised its ~~vermicute~~ vermiculated pale back, from Mary's book) perched on the Portugal-laurel, but alas! The cockerell chased it away. I polished Great Aunt Judith's long-case clock. She would have been 96 tomorrow, were it not for the mishap, with the PIGLET.

To coales.......10ᵈ Had a headache today

Great Aunt Judith. ~~Her bonnets were quite the thing, &~~ in her youth, she was a great FLIRT!!!

April 4<u>th</u> - no 5<u>th</u>

The little ragged boy called, & offered to despatch the Cockerell, but I thought him too young for the task, and explained that the Cockerell's execution was stayed, until the arrival of some guests (tho' blushing the while at my untruth.)

The child then told me of a strange ~~mallardy~~ malady very common in this part of the country ; an infection of the feet, heralded by a strange itching, and concluding, with the loss of all the toes, which drop off and are petrified, to the hardness of granite. He showed me 2 pebbles in his pocket, which he declared to be his sister's great-toes! Though I stared at his tale, I proceeded after his departure, to BOIL all dear W<u>ms</u> boots — which, the boy told me was the only remedy. The loss of dear W<u>ms</u> toes would be a terrible disaster.

Imagined my Beloved, so used to striding across the skyline, reduced to a mere hobble ! Tho' I resolved, should the worst happen, to keep dear William's toes in a little silk bag, tied around my neck.

Saved lettuce, beans & ~~braggery~~ bryony.

<u>To Prevent Fell - foot</u>

Boil the Boots, for 2 hours together, with a pinch of Plutonium. (Luckily I had some in my apron pocket !)

April 6th

William has gone for a long, & solitary walk.
It thrills my heart to think of him striding out
upon turf where, perhaps, no foot before has trod!

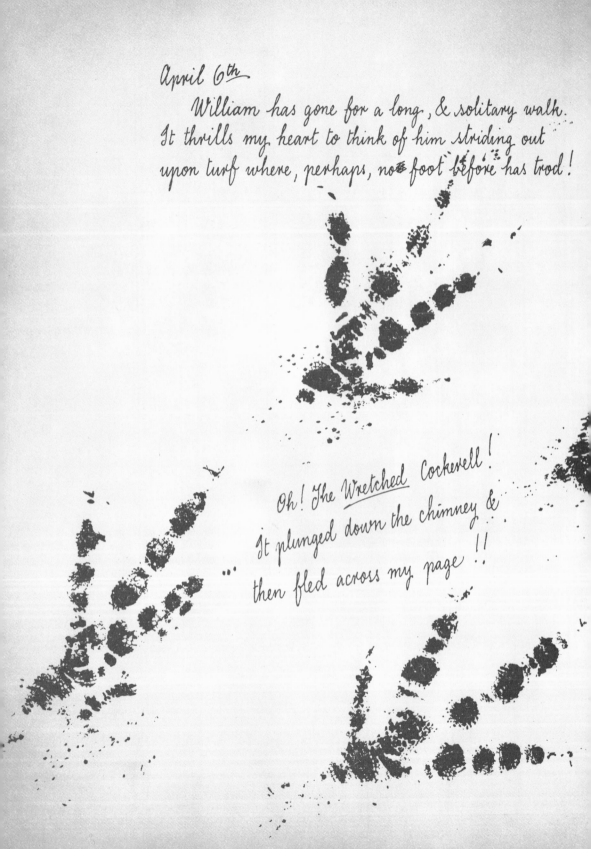

Oh! The Wretched Cockerell!
It plunged down the chimney &
... then fled across my page !!

Could you supply a bushel of goats' dung to Vole Cottage for a farthing, Fellow?
William has such a Natural Sympathy with the Common People
I could drap it on yeir heid for nothin, Hoity-Toity
SP

April 6th

This day Wm walked from Clobbercrack
Fell to Hammerhead Trout and back, taking
in the Crummocks : a distance of near 42 miles !!
What a thing is masculine vigour ! And perhaps
the ~~boyling~~ boiling of the boots proved beneficial.

A fine rain this evening. Cooked a plumb-
tart with last yrs. plumbs, bottled.

Dung delivered.

April 7th

Swept & scrubbed floors, polished the
furniture, washed the windows with an infusion of
Eyebright and Elder, & carted a prodigious quantity
of Dung up the bank, away from dear William's
windows. Starched his shirts after tea.

April 8th   Wm came to me in his shirt-sleeves
& with an expression of perplexity clouding
his features.

-Dorothy.- he said — is this shirt <u>starched</u>,
or not ?—

— Why yes William — I replied — I starched it
yesterday. Is it not well done ?—

My
Pickering Poke-
Bonnet.

—No, my dear sister—(always so affectionate, even in rebuke)—Starched? Call you this <u>starch^d</u>?— It's <u>limp</u>! it languishes. Pray remember Dorothy: You cannot over-starch for me. Always remember, my dear—that I wish to <u>crackle</u>.—

I was grateful for this clarification of his wishes. Dear William is so helpful in matters of domestic detail! A moment later he was observing that our omelettes (of peewit's eggs—offered at our door by the ragged boy, who said, there was a plague of peewits in Penrith—great clouds of them—the church spire had quite <u>buckled</u> under the weight of peewits, etc.—but I digress) ... as to the omelettes, W^m observed that an omelette was not edible, unless it had been fried for a quarter of an hour upon a fierce flame, and had attained the consistency of an <u>old purse</u>. I refried his omelette for ½ an hour, at which he appeared satisfied, the angel! Sowed Sow-thistle, Dog's Mercury & Long-Rooted Cat's Ear.

To Peewit's Eggs .... 2^d

Profile of the Little Ragged

Boy.

Alas! The soot is everywhere.

April 9th

    High winds: the Cockerell, ~~seeking~~ refuge from the storm, committed several nuisances upon the Kitchen-table. A tremendous fall of soot in the kitchen, coated our entire domestic offices, in deepest black – All my ~~baking~~ bread & cakes, spoiled. I was forced to fly to Mrs Grindstone, & beg a few crusts. Good Soul! She gave me, of her own make, a splendid <u>Cumberland-sausage</u>, of such a great girth, that William observed it resembled nothing so much as one of the snakes of Tropical Brazil.

    – This is what coomes – pronounced Mr Grindstone, of <u>book-larnin'</u>: Head in a book, nowt in't cupboard! —I mentioned the fall of soot, but to no purpose.

    – Head in a book – continued the old Dame – Auld Nick in't chimney! This is what coomes o' your hoity-toity ways, young lady –

    Blushing I deferred to her superior wisdom. –What you need, Miss Wordsmith – she cried as I departed —is <u>a maid of all work!</u> —

    – Alas, – I replied – dear Mrs Grindstone, our

How like the rings on the trunk of a felled tree!

political principles forbid such a thing! Equality
and fraternity, among all mankind, is our ideal:
to employ another for our daily tasks, would be to
demean a fellow-creature! —
—Hoity-Toity, and Scabberty-Wabberty! —
rejoined our neighbour, & withdrew, leaving me
in the lane, pondering upon her wise words.

April 10th

    Cleaned & scrubbed pantry, baked bread
& pies, bottled bluebells, starched W^{ms} handkerchiefs, patched his great coat, where the weasel's
teeth had torn it; dusted the coal-hole, & polished
the boulders, by the back-door; then banged the
mattresses upon the sod-wall, new lined the
counterpanes, & sowed Swine's-Cress, Stork's-bill
& Sneezewort — but William worked.
A new lyric: The Mad Vagabond. He will make a
copy for me here:

Swine's
Cress

I walked upon a Mountain road
And met an aged man
Who said "My head is full of owls!"
And capered, as he ran

He ran, & threw his hat about
And cried "God Bless the Snake!"
He kiss my hand, then daring plunged
Into the nearby lake.
Half-starved & mad, he swam & swam
Towards the setting sun
I, feeling awed and overcome
Sat down & ate a bun.
I fed some to the Little Stint
'Twas far more tame than he
He vanished in a pool gold
And I went home for tea.

So affecting! At the first reading, I wept, for half
an hour together. And then, struck by a thought,
I asked William if a ~~female~~ female vagabond, might not
be ~~rescued from~~ a life of misery, by the offer of
~~a place as Maid of All Work. Alas!~~ William
(oh! this dreadful pen! Thank G—; it did not
~~fall~~ blot upon dear William's sacred stanzas!)

be rescued from a life of misery, by the offer of
a place as Maid of all Work.
    Alas! William took the idea so ill, as to shout
at me! (O Heaven!) —

— My dear sister ! — he cried — if we cannot
ourselves execute the few humble duties needed to
sustain our life of modest comfort, what hope is
there for the Revolution ? If you require any
assistance in a daily task, I am entirely at your
disposal — and with that, he rose and brushed
the breadcrumbs from his waistcoat with such
natural majesty, that tears of admiration mingled
on my cheek, with those of gratitude.

— But I must waste no further time in domestic
debate, my dear — he declared — dinner as usual,
at half-past twelve —
   And he strode out into the lane, intent on solitary
contemplation of The Mad Vagabond.
   Composing in the wildness of Nature has always
been a passion with him, & I returned to my
pastry, refreshed by the glimpse of his dear
shoulders vanishing beyond the hornbeam.

   No sooner was my Dog's Mercury up, than it
was pecked to pieces by a Ptarmigan !

April 11th

    Mrs Grindstone called upon us, so early in the morning, we were all at sixes & sevens: Wm washing his feet in a bowl of water, upon the kitchen-table; I was endeavouring to extract the Cockerell from the depths of my night-shift, into which it had made a sudden dart.

    The fire was not lit, & the parlour floor was covered with _The Mad Vagabond_. Mr G. surveyed our ménage with a pursed lip, & observed dryly, that she had always concluded her domestic duties by 8am; had swept the flagstones, baked the bread etc, by then.

    I did not know what to offer her: too early for Whortleberry Cordiall, & one could scarcely insult her with the mouldy remnants of her own sausage. In the end I gave her a copy of _The Mad Vagabond_, perceiving too late, alas! that she could not read. She purs'd her lip & observed, that there were mad vagabonds enough abroad, without encouraging them by literature.

    However, she remarked, paper is always usefull, & to my relief, rose to go.

Wrote to
Cholericke
Jelley
John Pearse
Mary H.
Aunt Alice
The Dreadful Pitt!
Humphrey Davey
J. de Quinine

William
W. W.
Willie
Willy
Bill
Billie
Will

April 13th

Commencement of Iris's domestic regime, which she celebrated by sharpening the wooden spoons, & strangling the Cockerell.

— My owd mother did always say, I had a good arm for a stranglin' missus — she confided. This was reassuring I suppose..... I am not sure. For dinner, an excellent Cock a Leekie soup, tho' I do wish, that Iris had removed the beak & feet, ere committing the creature to the pot.

~~May~~ April 14th (tho' warm enough for May! Iris stripped to her bust-bodice whilst besoming the back steps. Luckily Wm & Mr P. both out.)

William reported a strange dream this morning, of a great Cumberland-sausage, steam pouring from its snout, tunnelling at great speed ~~from~~ through the mountains towards us!

Caught a Little Bustard, this evening, nibbling at my turnip-tops! Did not know whether to rejoice or despair. It rose up and seemed to rattle & hiss at me as it flew off.

The Stinking Hellebore is out.

Iris

April 15th

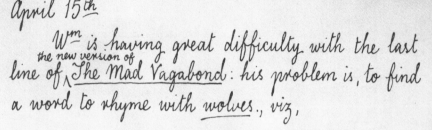

W.^m is having great difficulty with the last line of the new version of <u>The Mad Vagabond</u>: his problem is, to find a word to rhyme with <u>wolves</u>., viz,

> His eye was wild, his coat was torn
> His gait was slow & stiff
> I wondered where he had been born —
> Under some beetling cliff?
> And had he drunk of mother's milk
> Or supped from dugs of wolves?
> Or others of that feral ~~milk~~ ilk
> ··· — (here is the difficulty.) — ···

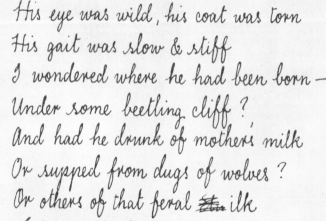

I suggested, W.^m should replace <u>wolves</u> with <u>foxes</u>. The last line then could be concluded, with a reference to boxes, or Cox's, or Doxeys, or Po—es, or Soxes, etc etc. But W.^m rejects the foxes, as not terrible enough for his purposes. And G— knows, his art is beyond my meagre powers to assist. I have, however, made 24 copies of the as yet incomplete lyric. We must ask Cholericke. .

Iris says a wild woman of the hills, Wise Ursula, is famous for her embrocation! W.^m went out to seek her, & returned much relieved.

April 16th

Our own mad Vagabond called today! The
Fellow who brings the letters. He is also engaged in
the cultivation of leeches: Wm bought 2¾d worth
today, as the fellow seemed to foresee some sick-
ness. He has the gift, he tells us, of second sight,
& indeed he often seems to anticipate the contents
of our letters with remarkable accuracy.
Today he brought news of Cholericke's imminent
arrival!! Tidings which filled us both with the
deepest joy!

Alas, it seemed the Leech Pedlar had had some
previous acquaintance, with Iris, for as he passed
the kitchen window, she flew out, & buried a
wooden spoon in his shoulder-blade, crying out
Swamp-Gurnet! He whirled about, & calling down
a bitter curse upon her (The Curse of Cockermouth,
I think it was) leapt over the turnips & was gone.

I had a word with Iris about the undesir-
ability of followers, & thought I had expressed
myself with delicacy & forbearance, but she took
it v. ill, and flounced off to the scullery, where

The Leech
Pedlar

To leeches,
three farthings

she banged about, and flung bits of cold Cockerell out of the window, just as W^m was passing on the gravel walk. I removed the giblets from his eye-brows (which were strangely glistening, for the rest of the day.) and was struck by the happiness of this accident. — For — I cried, does not Cholericke doat upon Giblet - Pie? I shall make one, after dinner. —

At that moment dinner appeared, Iris issuing into the garden, with a steaming tray.

— Aye aye — she observed — I do see that ye gentle-folks like to eat i' the open air, God save us! If ye'd spent as many nights as I have wi' not so much as a thornbush to shelter ye from t'hail and snow, ye'd not hold your roof in such contempt —

It chanced, at this moment, to start to rain, but we felt that we must eat outdoors, for the preservation of our domestic authority.

W^m munched on with philosophicall resign-ation, the rain streaming down his face.

April 17th

At 8 the Leech Pedlar brought us a letter from dear Mary, telling of great crouds of toads upon the roads in Yorkshire — no one knows why.

At 10, W^m put on his great coat, saying with an odd exhilaration in his eye,

— I think I will essay the potency once more of wise Ursula's _Embrocation_ — and was gone.

I was sitting alone, _Paradise Lost_ on my knee, when I heard a step outside, flew to the door — it was Cholericke!

I flung myself upon his bosom!

— My dear! — he cried — Good morning, good afternoon, good evening, or good night! Whichever is appropriate! —

Toads have always Exerted a strange fascination over me.

I felt at once, with his first words, the exhilaration of his organ of imagination. Such infinite space between those pale brows! And yet there seemed something hot & clammy about dear Cholericke, as I helped him over the doormat, which alarmed me—

Dear Cholericke is Arrived!

— Are you feverish? I enquired.

— When am I not feverish? — cried he, flinging

himself upon the sopha — He began to search thro' his
pockets, & brought out a little brown bottle, to my
Entire Alarm, having on previous occasions witness'd
~~the sort of intoxication~~ but loyalty forbids!! I offered
tea, and Giblet-Pie, but he declared he required
nothing, until William's return, but horizontality.

He had walked, he said, from Somerset in five
days, passed a coach stuck in a mire outside Birming-
ham, glimpsed the new manufactories at Stoke, &
heard a whole countryside of cuckows, crying, —in
the summer.

I enquired as to the health of Sara and the babes,
whereat poor Cholericke screamed, banged his head
against the fender, and then turned his great dark
eyes upon me, so that I almost boyled, in the
brilliancy of his Fancy.

He caught ~~his~~ my hand — I must tell you,
Dorothy — I must — yes — unburden myself to you —
you above all women — he urged!

My heart shook, my Imagination reeled, & I
almost sank under the waves of Possibility &
Impossibility!

— I love another! — he cried — ah the Chaos, Dorothy,

Part of dear
Cholericke's
Route

Burmingham

Nightingales
heard here

Greesington

R. Stinkly

Stoke-by-
Thunder

Cuckows
here

R. Oare

Twiddlecum-
Fibblethwaite

R. Fassett

N

Pocklington
Parva

a Dodo, here
(can he mean
his wife?)

Nether Stowey

of the Human Condition! To be shackled to one,
and to long for Another!—

    And he gazed at me with such penetration, I
could only nod dumbly, as terror & amazement fled
thro' every vein!

    Her name is also <u>Sara</u> — he confided, at which
I seemed to fall into an abyss of deafness & black
despair, of whirling words and eddying feeling, &
'twas all I could do, to call out to Iris, to bring us
some toasted-muffins.

    My composure returned, & I found Cholericke
flushed, but still: gazing most attentively into my
face: purged (it seemed) by his confession.

    — Tell me, Dorothy,— he whispered suddenly—
have not you — pray, confess it: as I have in this
most unexpected — (he lowered his voice)—
& if I may say so, deliciously revealing tête-a-tête.
also confess'd, my dear—

    Do you and dear William ever ..... you know...
Pyramus & Thisbe ? .... Hero & Leander ? ......
Eros & Psyche ? —

Dorothy, In glancing o'er your journal, I could not help noticing
you employ the frustian old <u>dash</u>—to punctuate speech. This is
quite outmoded, my dear— & I must entreat you to embrace
the <u>Inverted Comma</u>, In future thus: "Yes William!"

I was happy to give dear Cholericke an account of our recent reading &, to enquire after his own, but he seemed distracted, tossed to & fro upon the sopha, and at length, declared he would surrender himself to the Newtonian Principle, & rolled onto the floor, where, beneath the table, he became at last still and contemplative.

At this moment dear Wᵐ returned, & our jubilation at being all three re-united, was reinforced by the sharing of the Giblet-Pie, & by William's reading us a lyrical fragment he composed this morning : —— Upon a Dunghill.

— All to bed exhilarated. Slept till noon.

April 18th

Sat in the orchard & talked. Cholericke much exercised over Locke's Essay Concerning Human Understanding.

Wᵐ dreamt of a sea of boiling slugs. Jack-by-the-Hedge & the London Rocket, both up.

April 19th Cholericke is out gathering herbs, for a tisane.

April 20th This day has entirely pass'd from my recollection.

Wᵐˢ Hand:
No Heart line!
& No Mount of Venus!
(Quite relieved, somehow!)
All Head & Destiny!

Head
Destiny

Heart
Love
Imagination

Cholericke's Hand
Large Mons Veneris!
& Imagination!
Bifurcated heart line!
(Ink stains not significant)

April 17th or 16th

Forget which. We walk, talk, read & write. Sat with Cholericke in the orchard till 3 am. Wm slipped on a toad & banged his head.

April 20th   The bliss of our retired life here most sweetly evident to us, and we all 3 rejoice in the spring unfolding in field & hedgerow. Iris's domestick exertions, tho' often strange, freeing me for Poetick Contemplation.   Made 25 copies of _Upon a Dunghill_, and talked with C. about Understanding. What is _Brain_, and what is _mind_? Were one a Materialist — but dear me! The bleak Atheisticall blankness, of a world simply running along, like a machine without a driver!! _Horror_!!! And yet ~~so simpl~~ — but still ~~~~ —

I cannot ~~cont~~ —————

I fear I have taken too much Hawthorn Tea!! Cholericke brought it & makes it for us, insisting on its power to inflame the imagination and drive out Phallusg ᴵPhallacy (—strange,! I cannot spell it)— fear my Brain (or is it my Mind?) tired out with too much _Metaphysical Speculation_ — Head full of Music. Giddy. To _Bed_!

Dorothy — I am in the Orchard — Cxxx

Bring a bottle :: two!!

Head of Venus

Order
Ham
Cloves
Arrowroot
Brains

April 21st I think.

    Today, Cholerike was very exhilarated, & read us *Orlando* ~~the~~ *Furioso*, with breaks only for sandwiches, claret, & trips to the N———

(I fear the nostrils are not quite right, tho' W^m thinks the knees rather fine !!)

Alas! In a moment of great excitement, Cholericke knocked over the inkwell.

Strange ! C. says the blot looks like the ghost of an Albatross !!

Went to bed at 4am. (Cholericke insisted on finishing the work). V.V. weary. Could not but wish we had retired _earlier_. The bolsters are quite musty, & need airing, but I have been a truant, to domestic duties, for many days.

Here, Cholericke set
down his little brown
bottle. It looks a little
like the _rising_ _sun_, does it not?

But the _moon_ would be more appropriate....
the moon which makes men mad. Alas! Poor C.!!

The next day. (Not sure of date) Slept, & was v. ill.

The day after. C. talks of going on a tour to the Highlands. We are encouraging him, in this plan of his.

Some of the Little Brown Bottle, _spilt_
Hardly dare to sniff the page!

April or May. Forget which.

Today it rained incessantly, & we were all ill. Walked over Helvellyn and heard the hoarse grunt of the Great Bustard! Returned soaking wet. Cholericke retired to the sopha, declaring he had taken a fever, and was much troubled with an inflammation of the ———s, an unwelcome relapse, he told us, of an ancient malady. He begged me to cover him with our servicable old horse-blanket, so that he could scratch himself, without offending the company — whilst still hurling himself with undiminished vigour, into the conversation. Poor soul! He dictated 2 letters to Miss Sara ——— whilst Wᵐ was shaving above. Dear me! Cholericke's arrival has thrown so many puzzling questions to the fore-front of my poor, vexed mind!!

End of April, approx — Suspect that domestic disorder is taking hold of our humble abode. Though Iris does her best, she has some strange notions.

Today, for instance, she soaked the bacon in ~~tar~~ ~~~~ but no matter. Resolve that when dear Cholericke leaves us, as he promises to, for his tour

Reading-List
(Cholericke's
suggestion)
Albertus Magnus
Cornelis Agrippa
von Nettesheim
Paracelsus
Frederick von Spee
All re: Magic &
Astrology!

♀ ☿ ☽

△ ♀

☊ ○ ☉

♎

♉ magic
symbols
♁ (Must not
tell Wᵐ!)

*Digitalis
Purpurea*

of the Highlands, I will perform a Spring-cleaning and give Iris more precise instruction in the arts of household-management.

St. Norman's Day.—so the Leech Pedlar informs me. As I write, C. is annotating Locke beneath the horse-blanket upon the sopha; W^m staring into the fire, revolving in his mind the impression made upon his Phancy this morning, of a broken wall; myself am translating Xenophon into Cumberland dialect. Such a deep sense of peace and harmony pervades our dear cot! Only the scratching of my pen (& of Cholericke beneath the horse-blanket, poor soul!); the crackle of the fire, & the occasional crash from the scullery, encroach upon a perfect *living* stillness of love, & schollarship.

*Sowed Foxgloves today
Such a shame
the darlings
are so
poisonous!*

May 1st

Words can scarce express the ~~turm~~ turmoil into which our humble household has been thrown!

I write these words by moonlight in the linen-cupboard, which must be my bed tonight, for,

LORD BYRO is ARRIVED !!!

May 2nd

In the Pantry. Scarce time or leisure to write a word! Lord Byro has bought with him a young cousin (or so he claims –) one Teresa Sanseveria – an Italian girl, though dressed as a boy, in the uniform of Harrow-School (Puzzling!) Signorina S. ~~is~~ is v. ill & strangely corpulent, and has retired to bed, & Iris

To Order
Cloves
Pigs Cheeks
~~Cocoa~~ (Cocoa)
Pickled Gherkins
Powdered
Pumice-Stone

May 3rd

Was surprised then, by Lord B, who thrust himself insolently into the pantry, & threw me backwards with such abandon, I sat upon a block of pigs lard & quite _ruined_ my skirt! (Iris recommends that we coat the rest of the skirt with pigs lard, likewise thus providing me with a v. serviceable waterproof!) Dear Iris! She is so full of real virtues, despite her eye!

To Order.
Urgent
Pigs Lard

2 pm. (written under the table) Iris informs me, that Signorina S. is in labour, in William's bed !! Thrown by this news into a vortex of anxiety. Where will my darling sleep tonight ? (Last night, he walked all night, on Scatterbone Pass.)

And what will become of the Signorina ? And the child ? — As for Lord B...... the v. moment we met, he kissed my hand with such abandon, I had to soak it in turpentine for 2 hours afterwards, to dispel the tingling. I must go and boil water for Iris.

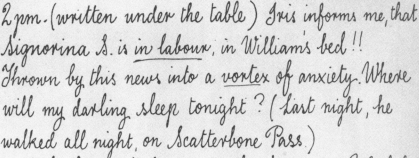

Signorina Sanseveria

10 pm. Signorina S. still labouring above. Her groans are terrible to hear, & vibrate strangely in the long-case clock.

Lord Byro seems not at all perturbed: he sits with Cholericke, sipping soda-water & eating biscuits, & talking of Italy.

W^m refuses to speak to him, & has gone off to climb Clatteringshaws, with a piece of pork in his pocket.

I dart from hiding-place, to hiding-place, but whenever C. drops into a doze, — I am in danger from Lord B.

Lord
Byro
Alas, 'tis not
Satanick
enough.

2 am ~~this~~ In the orchard, lurking under
our ~~gro~~ gnarled old Lord Lambourn. I write in the dark,
having sought sanctuary here from Lord Byro's
incessant importunities. He pursued me, the moment
that Cholericke slept, <u>67</u> times around the house.

Even now I hear him panting & plunging
among the cabbages in the kitchen-garden
below.

But if I hold my Brea

This page I leave Blank:
Monument to a Disgraceful
Episode. D.W.

May 4th 11am.

Lord Byro leapt upon me last night, in the orchard! My poor journal was _thrust_ _face down_ upon the earth: myself _tumbled upon_ it, his L'ship flung himself upon me, & were it not for the fact that he cracked his head upon the apple-tree trunk, & lay insensible for ~~some~~ some minutes, I should have been quite _undone_ !!!

Signora S. still in labour. I tried to assist Iris, ~~but~~ but the anguish of the poor Signorina too much for my nerves. If only C. would awake, or Wm return! I am safe nowhere: and am at present hiding in The _Water-Butt_, holding my journal above the surface, &

Oh! I dropt it in!

Profile of Lord B.

(His dreadful physiognomy seems to exert an awful Fascination over me!)

Dear Dorothy,

Would you be good enough to starch & set out my Fell-Trousers, together with a piece of Pickled Pork, at 3am. I shall ascend Shivering Riggs tomorrow, via the Devil's Danglers.

I must observe, I am surprised to find that you consider the above sketch an appropriate adornment for your Journal, Which I had hitherto regarded as a mine of Poetic Inspiration and Good Sense.

yrs. Wm

NB Please do not meddle with my Boots in the night

Oh Heaven! Wm has honoured my poor journal with one of his inspired notes! & was offended by my sketch of the appalling Byro!! I am weeping uncontrollably upon the Pickled Pork!!!

4 pm. This afternoon I was hiding from Lord B: I was folded up in the long-case clock. When Lord B. entered the parlour, the door of the clock swung open !! Lord B. gazed upon me from across the room, his eyes glowing like coals.

"Dear Miss W!" he cried, "So delectable, even folded up in a clock!"

"I was just oiling the mechanism, My Lord," I explained, & scrambled out, all a-tremble.

"Ah Dorothy!" he growled with a wolvish grin. "My dear! Will not you do the same for me?" And he shot me a look of such electric magnetism that my stays snapped, my jet necklace fused, & a fork of lightning zig-zagged down my bodice, at which all my mother-of-pearl buttons burst from my bosom, & bounced upon the floor.

"I am undone!" I cried

"What kind co-operation!" murmured Lord B. in a satanic undertone, sidling around the sopha towards me (O Heaven! Must I remember !?)

"Come to my arms, Cara Mia!" breathed the

dreadful Lord B., & at another flash from his eyes, all the metal objects in the room, buckled & bent: the fingers of the clock twisted into a knot, the windows opened by themselves with an unearthly scream, & as luck would have it, the hook on the ceiling slowly uncurled, dropping a large ham upon the sleeping form of dear Cholericke upon the sopha——

"Dear Sara!" he cried, half awake, & embracing the ham with great familiarity, "Let us seize the moment! Kiss me, my Angel! But not too loudly! My wife is in the next room!"

At which Lord B. laughed so loud, it brought Cholericke to his senses: they began to talk about rhyme, & free verse, & I escaped to the kitchen, where I am writing this. What chaos has gripped our humble house, since Lord B. fell, like a Comet, upon us! The screams of his unfortunate companion still ring in my ears: the knives & forks are all bent beyond belief; and (I forgot to mention this earlier) the peacocks & baboons he brought in his coach, have laid waste my dear vegetable garden, & insulted Mrs Grindstone, as she passed in the lane, by presenting their ———— to her.

. But where is William ? I do hope that the pocketful of pork will be sustaining enough for my darling.

May 5th

Signorina S. delivered at 4am. of a fine daughter. Iris officiated. The child to be named Aphrodite.

Cholericke commiserated with Byro upon the sex of the babe, saying that to his mind, Childe & Man Childe were synonymous:

Damme I love the sex tho' Chole, retorted his L-ship, rolling an eye at me; ——— the scoundrel !!

May 6th

I have hopes that now Lord Byro's companion is safely delivered, they may agree to remove — perhaps to rent a house in Ambleside, which may prove more congenial to Milord's cosmopolitan tastes.

He has not pursued me above 6 times today: his ardour seems to be cooling.

Iris has a sly look. I hope she has not been lured into indiscretion. Wm sleeps in the wash house with Mr Pickerel, who has taken Lord B's likeness several times & is now sketching the outline of his magnificent Phaeton.

To new cutlery 1s 6d
To new ceiling-hook . . . . ¼d
To new window catches 2s 11d
To new Mother of Pearl buttons . . 3d
To new stays 1s 6d

Lord B. is proving an expensive guest! Wm seems v. ill tempered, & cross with me, at the moment.

A letter from Mary Hutchinson, with paper-patterns for Easter Bonnets (rather too late!)

Dear Doro! When you read this, I'll be gone, I fear
We leave for Venice, where I have some bills to pay
But you'll be bright & clear within my mind, my dear
From now until at least a week next Wednesday.
I kissed you in the Orchard & upon the Stair
But coy & nimble, you escaped me — like no other
It drives me mad to think of your bright eyes & hair
All wasted on that Fossil-Fish, your Brother
    Have pity on me now! My dear Miss W!
    Elope with me & he no more will trouble you.

Alas! I know your answer, & must bid Farewell
Though taking with me one poor souvenir of you
Which I shall cherish to the very Gates of Hell
I mean the Pig's Lard, destined for some dreadful Stew
On which I thrust you, panting, t'other night
It still, my angel, bears th'imprint & lovely shape
Of your most noble Fundament! — I swoon! — The sight
Too touching, Dearest! You, the angel! I, the ape!
    I trembling kiss the Lard, & think of you
    Here are my Lips: I bid a Glistening Adieu

Byro

Farewell

May 7th

Good G——!.. Lord Byro, has had the insolence to write in my Journal, & leave the Impression of his Vile Lips upon the Page !!!

I can scarce contain my Fury! I Shake, & feel myself really _Swooning Away_

Still, at least he is Gone Away! Taking his Signorina, the sweet babe &, I am glad to say, _most_ of the Baboooons (one ran away into Lowther's Wood & has not been seen since.)

Iris is crying in the Pantry, & will not tell me why. I cannot leave off reading his wretched stanzo's & tho' I wish to tear the page out & fling it upon the fire, I know not why.... I feel a strange paralysis of the will. Cholericke is insensible upon the rag-rug: Wm is cheerful. I must be busy: I must occupy myshelf myself.

I shall go and _scald his Sheets_ !

Good G——! I appear to have lost control of my _Doodles_ !

May 20th

I have been unable to write my journal for many days: was seized with a strange fever, & palpitations; voices in my head — mostly baritone ones, alas! urging me to depravity. Am now slightly recovered.

Iris has propped me in an old apple box, by the door, to take the air. Too weak to write more.

Will tear Lord B—'s poem out, when my strength returns. The Wild Arum is out.

Wild Arum or Lords &—Oh!

May 21st The scent of the Hawthorn drifts past me in my apple box. How I long to bury my face in the sweet flowers of the Spring!

Wm & C. walked up the Gorkeys today, & William brought me back a ~~sweet~~ fantastical fossil. Buried my face in the fossil, instead.

Black Byrony Bryony O Heaven!

May 22nd Well enough to walk around the house, but v. distressed at the state of the kitchen: cocoa in the coal-scuttle, giblets in my sewing-box, etc. Iris says she has a system, & I am too weak to argue. Wm got wet feet, on Flabbergoat Fell.

May 23rd

Banged a few bolsters today, upon the wash-house house wall, & felt much better for it.

Mr Pickerell presented me with a sketch of a primrose: so kind!

May 24th Have resolved never to think of Lord B. again and will burn his poem, tomorrow.

Iris sick, this morning. Wm & C. also unwell. Myself feel stronger daily.

May 25th Strong enough to visit Mrs Grindstone today. Found her coating her stays with calf's foot jelly. "Nowt like it for t'rheumatics," she observed, & assured me she could also glide most harmoniously into them, so lubricated.

Went home, and coated Wm's boots with calf's foot jelly, as I have always feared the rheumatism.

May 26th William slipped upon the doorstep, & broke his head against the doorpost. Much mortified thereat: anointed his head with remains of the calf's foot jelly, & put him to bed, but he slipped off the pillow.

Heart's Ease
(Applied some
to mine
externally —
but no
discernable
effect)

To bandage
the skull
apply Vinegar
& brown paper
to the contusion:
wrap securely
round with
copper wire
attached to ears

May 27th

All much better today — except Iris, who sat shuddering over the stewpan.

William, Cholericke & I walked up Flabberghast Pass and ascended the Bonkins. Fine views from the Left Bonkin (known locally as The Witches ————). We could see as far as the Isle of Man, though I was unable to discern the exact form of the bonnets of the Manx ladies. Alas, I fear my eyesight is deteriorating!

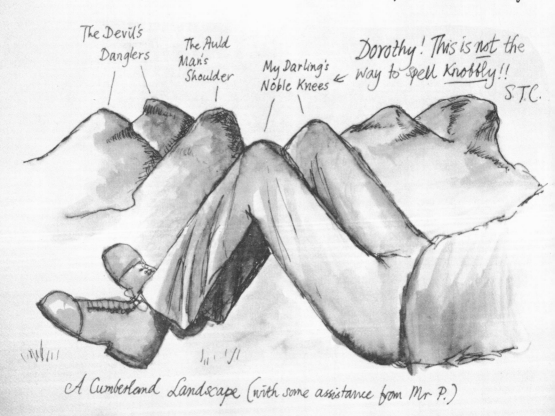

The Devil's Danglers

The Auld Man's Shoulder

My Darling's Noble Knees

Dorothy! This is not the way to spell Knobbly!!

S.T.C.

A Cumberland Landscape (with some assistance from Mr P.)

(W^m thinks
the hair
too thin)

Ah

On the Subjects of the Original Corruption
of our Nature, the doctrines of Redemption,
Regeneration, Grace & Justification by Faith,
my Convictions are altogether different from
those of Drs Priestley, Lindsey, & Disney.

Cholericke praised, above all human Virtues, generosity.
Inspiring! But then he mentioned the Impossibility of
his departing for the Highlands without some financial
assistance. Then, embarrassed, he all of sudden leapt
across the abyss dividing us from the ~~left~~ Right Bonkin,
only stumbling a little as he landed, & crying
"I'll see you at home my dear friends! Pray forgive!"
he plunged into the mists.

W^m & I took a sweet walk home, my head on his
shoulder, his hand on my tippet.

We talked seriously about the possibility of

Here be my flamin' DUMPLINGS, Missus
What rhymes with DUMPLINGS?
Y'know, Dorothy when I think of you, I always think, if one had been expecting a PLAIN woman, one would be AGREEABLY SURPRISED
Sometimes I think I love William best, & sometimes, Cholericke
SP

Cholericke's departure : W^m convinced, that if he is ever to complete his new lyrics (The Blasted Thorn, The Mad Gorse-Gatherer, The Hole in the Wall, & the Solitary Stone — inspiring!) he must enjoy a little more domestick peace & quiet, which might be provided by the temporary departure of dear Cholericke for Scotland. But alas! We have no funds.

W^m proposed, that I should add to our Exchequer by taking in washing and mending, and perhaps in my moments of leisure, doing some tatting or lace-making or the like.

I readily agreed to all this, & upon our return home I summoned the little Ragged Boy, desiring him to make known this new work of mine, to the neighbourhood.

Not ten minutes later, he arrived back with a large parcell, requesting that I mend Mrs Grind-stone's stays. Alas! So intractable was the material, that I was forced, to hire a local carpenter to make good the stays, with strips of elm, which cost 2s 6d.

So we begin our new venture out of pocket.

May 28th

V. busy all day washing, ironing & starching.
Up all night tatting hessian antimacassers.
Too tired to write more. Iris v. ill & lethargic.

To Order
(for Laundering)

Liquid Ammonia
Ox-gall
Rottenstone
Linseed Oil
Fine Sand
Blacklead
Paraffin
Fuller's Earth
Slaked Lime
Silver Sand
Starch
Wax Candles
Turpentine
Borax
Emery Powder
Oxalic Acid
Liquid Gum
Pure Alcohol
Blue
Epsom Salts
Yellow Soap
Soda, Bleach
Glycerine, Benzine
Alum-Water

May 29th   More washing came today - including
Mrs Grindstone's night-shifts, which seemed to
smell of brimstone. Cholericke, lying upon the sopha,
made a jest about witches, that I thought in poor
taste.
Wm walked up Pobblestacks & returned inspired.

May 30th   Came down this morning to find Iris
eating my antimacassars!
She could not explain this aberration. I seized the
remainder, & gave them to the Little Ragged Boy,
to take to Ambleside market & sell for me.
He returned at dusk empty handed, saying
they had been pecked to bits by Kestrels.
V. disconsolate. Things go badly! Although
the Little Ragged Boy did not look so ragged,
tonight. — So glad. Poor creature.

← Am apprehensive, as to these Necessities.

May 31st

    Iris is become very lazy and dull, so that I have to perform all the domestic duties, as well as the washing, ironing,, starching and tatting.

    W^m asked me to make 150 copies of <u>The Solitary Stone</u>, & was not very satisfied, with the quality of my work: my hand still <u>shook</u> from the incessant tatting.

    Poor William! I wept to disappoint him so, & endeavoured to improve matters, by holding the pen with both hands.

    Cholericke is reading Byro's <u>Childe Harolde</u>. I wish he would not.

    <u>The Solitary Stone</u> (one last copy, for myself)

What mysteries has thou seen, O Stone?
Amongst the scree of Flabberghast, alone
Patiently enduring rain & hail & snow
For tens of thousand years, for aught I know.
The throb of centuries has left thee blank
Until I plucked thee from the mountain's flank
To offer thee employment: by our door
It's better, now: it used to <u>bang</u>, before.

The Norfolk Nobbler

We could not identify this butterfly.

Wm says it is German

June 1st.

Have made £1·3s· 4½d from my extra work: gave it to Cholericke & suggested he might set out upon his long-postponed trip to Scotland. He kissed me gratefully, packed his bag, and departed. William and I basked in a strange unearthly calm all afternoon, and chased butterflies, as we had done years ago.

At 4pm. Cholericke returned, saying he had had an Idea (something we always dread), and muttering about sacred rivers, he collapsed upon the sopha, with a strange CLINK, & I found in his pocket, three new brown bottles! V. mortified. Instructed Iris to empty them, & refill with weak tea. Had a headache today. William washed his feet, & a butterfly perched on one, for a moment, in a ray of sunlight by the kitchen door! O fortunate insect! I think it was a Buckinghamshire Wobbler.

The Meadow Dodger

Small Brown Buggart

Buckingham Wobbler

June 2nd

Have suspended the washing, tatting, etc. as Cholericke's departure seems unlikely. He is beneath the table, as I write, & fairly quiet — only screams at intervals.

Am not sure what to do with the great mountain of laundering materials: the Liquid Ammonia, Ox-Gall, etc., but Iris assures me she can do something with the Paraffin & Glycerine. Rather sly about exactly what.

Mary Hitchinson writes boasting that her ARISARUM PROBOSCIDIUM is out. Not too far, I trust. Iris said today, that she liked the name Harold, for a boy. I told her I preferred William !!

Had a headache again today.

June 3rd

Awoken at 2 o'clock by the Leech-Pedlar's dreadful halloo: he brought us a letter announcing the imminent arrival of the poet PERCY JELLEY and his lady-love MARY GODWIT — Eloping !!

Did not know what to think. Wm has corresponded with Mr Jelley, & they greatly admire his work, so I said I would prepare their beds, & some breakfast, at once.

Sheep's Bit, or Hairy St Johns Scabious (Tho' I cannot believe St John was that hairy) Iris wears it in her bosom as she says it deters grasshoppers. Strange.

"That will be satisfactory, Dorothy", William concluded—"Welcome our guests, & if I have not come down by noon, you might bring me a little bread and milk". I eagerly agreed, W^m retired & Iris and I set about the preparation of as hearty a breakfast, as the weary pair were like to desire. Dismayed to find the pantry empty: what could we contrive? Iris undertook to sally forth & see what Nature might offer. She returned, only ½ an hour later, with the carcase of a fine jack-hare, she had surprised amongst the gorse. She had seized it, strangled it & skinned it, whilst walking home—& promised she would make William a fine fur-cap ~~with~~ of the skin, with the paws, as she put it,

"Two a-danglin' by his brows and two adown his neck, dearie."

Was not entirely convinced, that such a garment would be acceptable to my dear brother, but grateful for the thought. Iris boyled the hare, with holly-bark.

Not quite sure····

In the parlour, our arrangements were somewhat hampered by the sleeping form of poor Cholericke upon the sopha, whom the most urgent shakings failed to rouze.

Iris & I carried him into the wash-house, where Mr Pickerell was already up, sketching dew drops by moonlight. He received dear C. with eagerness, and arranged him (still unconscious) upon his bed of straw & sacks.

"I will strip him naked, dear ladies," cried Mr P. "and will take advantage of the moment, for a life-study — have had no such practice, since the Academy."

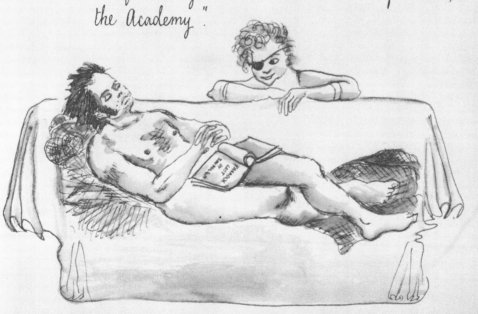

I'll help you, Sir!" cried Iris, seizing poor C.'s breeches and pulling hard, but I intervened, reminding Iris of the hare stew which required her best attention elsewhere.

She withdrew, but with a bad grace. I cannot but think she is possesst with a measure of _lewdness_, alas!

The sound of horses in the lane, heralded our guests, both mounted on one aged Nag: Mr Jelley in a sorry state, his arm in a sling; Miss Godwit pale, & beautiful.

She greeted me with the most touching courtesy.

Mr Jelley dismounted with difficulty.

"Alas, Miss W.," he lamented, "You will find me a very sad dog.— accidents rush upon me — Since commencing this elopement, I have twisted my anckle, & suffered a dislocation of my <u>Latissimus Dorsi</u>."

We led him to the sopha, where the poor soul lay quite still, his eyes closed, whilst Iris, Miss Godwit & I bathed his poor ankle, & anointed it with oil.

In the midst of our ministrations, Cholericke burst in — to my horror, <u>Stark-Naked</u>!— & cried "What? Mary Magdalene? Are there <u>three</u> of you, my dear? Or is it the effect of the Navelwort upon my <u>optick nerve</u>?"

I hurried him from the room, averting my eyes the while, which had the unfortunate result, that I banged my head upon the door post, so hard, that I saw stars, & almost fainted away.

Took poor C. back to the wash-house, where Mr P. in great consternation: he had slipt out, to the Necessary, and returned to find poor C. gone. He must have awakened in great distress of mind, poor C! ~~Though that is nothing~~

Percy Jelley
Poet, Atheist
& Eloper.

Mary Godwit
Feminest & Elopee.

Mr P. undertook to restore poor C. to lucidity: his confusion arose, we think, from an unwise infusion of _St Mary's Buttons_. From infusion to confusion! (V. diverting!!)

My guests now confessed themselves hungry: we accordingly set before them the dish of Boyled Hare. Mr Jelley leaned forward & peered at the dish.

— 'Tis a fine young _hare_ — I confided — which Iris strangled in the dark, not five hours since, & boyled —

— Good God! shrieked Mr Jelley, & then astonished me very much, by _vomiting into his great-coat pocket_!!

— Forgive us, dear Miss W! — cried his lady-love — we are vegetarians!

— Take the poor corpse away! — cried her consort — Out of my sight! ——

I instructed Iris to remove the hare, & to see if she could contrive some modest refreshment, without recourse to beasts of the field.

Whilst Iris was absent, Miss G. confided to me in an undertone, that poor Mr J. is much obsessed

Memo! cancel!
~~Hide~~ the
Calf's Head
Oxcheeks
Sweetbreads
Tripe
& Oysters.

The Onion
Upon which I must bend my Ingenuity

Spaggety-
Ferdy

An Italian
Dish

Iris also tells
me of other
Italian
Dishes:
Risotaugh
Pitser
Mac Aroney.
(scottish,
surely.)
and a baked
dish called
es Ennuie (?)
which I am
sure must
be French!

by death. His way of staring blankly at my sewing-
basket, as if it were the saddest sight on earth,
convinced me that the poor fellow was in a desperate
case. Am convinced, that his Atheism does not help.

Iris brought in an Italian dish, she had learned
off a sailor from Genoa, when she plyed her trade
in Whitehaven (tho' what her trade was, exactly.
I am at a loss to discover — I think she was a
laundress.)

'Twas a purely vegetarian dish, she promised,
known in Italy as Spaggety-Ferdy, and composed
of long strands, she declared was Horsetail (it
grows in my vegetable patch, next to the Fat Hen)

Mr Jelley managed a mouthful: Miss
Godwit, several, & I made an excellent breakfast,
being very hungry indeed.

After breakfast, Mr Jelley requested solitude:
I led him to my own bedroom (Cholericke was
asleep under the Yew-Tree) where he roamed about,
stared into space, and gazed thro' the window upon
the rocks beneath.

"How jagged those rocks are!" he exclaimed.

Saxifraga
Kamschatka

"Could one, do you think, leap from this window &
be sure of dashing one's brains out upon them?"

I reassured him immediately, ran downstairs &
covered the rocks with the sofa-cushions, & an old
Turkey carpet, but Mr Jelley's pale face at the window
still loomed in an ominous & melancholy way.

W^m came down, & Miss Godwit greeted him with
the most exquisite compliments: swore she always
carried The Ideot Sheep next to her heart, & prov'd
it by unbuttoning her bodice & tearing open her shift
—still, she is an anarchist, & they think nothing of
female modesty.

~~All the same I could not help feel~~ William offered
to give her a private recitation in the orchard: she
received the invitation with joy: they glided up the
garden-path, like two souls in Dante, rising
towards Paradise (& leaving me in the Stygian pit,
with Iris.)

Finding our cupboard bare, I sent Iris to Mrs
Grindstone to request assistance, tho' most reluctant
to reinforce the old dame's notions, of our domestic
anarchy.

Iris returned with a large Hasty-pudden, a Keswick
Curious-Cake, & a ~~Sagoe~~ dish of Sagoe, made with
shrew's milk. All impeccably vegetarian!

Whilst Iris absent, I lingered in the garden,
eavesdropping upon William's recitation, & suddenly
noticed, with what a qualm! — that the Jelley's old grey
horse had <u>quite lost its tail</u>.

Straight the discovery rushed in upon me, that our
Spaggedy Ferdy, the long strands of which had
mystified me, had been none other than the <u>poor</u>
<u>creature's rear adornment</u>!

Was sick behind the DODECATHEON (which is
doing v. well this year)

At 3pm. William descended from the garden &
consumed most of the boyled Hare, with evident con-
tentment. Then rising, he announced,

"I am going to show Miss Godwit The Grommets,
my dear Dorothy," —

I seized my coat, as the scenery about the
Grommets is especially beautiful, with a wildness
of rock and weather, exactly to my taste, but alas!

"I would be obliged if you would remain here, my

Keswick
Curious-Cake.

Marzipan   Lemon

Sponges

Choc.

almonds

Dried
Fruit

I know
not
what.

A simple
Peasant
Recipe

dear sister," he continued, "and minister to Mr Jelley & to poor Cholericke."

"Of course, William," I cried, instantly putting-off my coat, & I watched W^m & Miss Godwit disappear up the lane, with a strange burning in my throat — rushed indoors — buried my face in the washing-basket & cried for a full half hour. I know not why

Recovered myself — washed my face, in the rain-water barrel, & looked to my guests: Cholericke, now dressed, was deep in An Essay Concerning Human Understanding, Mr Pickerell ~~dressing~~ sketching him. Mr Jelley was asleep upon my bed, a great swathe of Aunt Judith's counterpane wound around his neck. I permitted myself a moment's repose and sat in the sunshine upon the doorstep: ate a morsel of the Curious Cake, admired the new shoots of the Rosa ~~Minor~~ Provincialis Minor, & felt, for a brief moment, quite ~~seri~~ serene.

—Iris v. torpid

What a strange Doodle I have made!

Dorothy
—it resembles the Medusa Head at the Arsenal, Berlin by Andreas Schlüter (1696) Can it be that you are a Re-incarnation?
Just a thought! C.xxx

Iris's
a Cordiall
against
Vipers

6 oz Monkshood
2 oz Henbane.
Handful
Laburnum-Seeds
10 Holly berries
5 leaves of Yew
Tuft of Hellebore
A handful of
Chopped
Foxgloves

Impeccably
Vegetarian,
Iris points out!
What can she
mean?

June 4th

Day of peace, and very beautiful soft grey clouds, hanging in the vale. Mr Jelley rested, gazing sadly upon my old gardening-boots: Iris was slumped under the mangle, & Cholericke beneath the Portugal-laurel

Mr P. sketched, saying he found Mr Jelley's ~~pof~~ profile, most striking: I was surprised, that an artist should seem indifferent to Miss Godwit's lovely face.

As for Miss Godwit · · · · very animated at breakfast (for which William was early, for once!) she begged him to show her his Withered Turnip, which he afterwards did, in the privacy of the orchard.

"Perhaps, my dear Miss Godwit," he suggested, "You may work with me upon it, & see if we can render it in a more perfect state."

At these words, I felt a most horrible stomach-qualm, as if struck, in the solar-plexus. William has never invited me to work upon his poems. But then, Miss Godwit is an Anarchist, & a Feminist, whereas I am nowt but a poor Household-Drudge.

Took juniper-tea, to disperse the Bile.

June 5th

Wm discomposed: took no breakfast & sulked, in the orchard alone. Mr Jelley, reviving, took Miss G. upon a ~~so~~ short horse ride as far as Slacktrusswater.

Whilst they were gone, I approached William, & asked him, what was the matter? It appeared that Miss Godwit had expressed discontentment with the conclusion of his Withered Turnip: found it premature, and weak.

"Damn the Reading Public!" he thundered. "If you write at length, they affect tedium: if your lyric is short, they are left unsatisfied."

I begged Wm to make a copy of The Withered Turnip in my journal, which he has consented to do:

Wm says,
It is not
Withered Enough

The Withered Turnip

It lay there wizened on the ground
Thro' rain & hail & snow
Four inches wide, of modest size
And hairy all below.
But no-one came to gather it
It knew no knife nor pot
It turned into a fossil-fruit
The Turnip all forgot

W.W.

What sublime simplicity! It makes me _weep_.
I expressed my astonishment, that anyone as discrimin-
ating as Miss Godwit could not have discerned the
perfection of form and energetic simplicity of <u>The
Withered Turnip</u>. I massaged William's neck, &
tempted him with some arrowroot and brandy. His
temper soon improved.

To Arrowroot
6d

     Felt better in my stomach, today.
An hour later: Oh the darling! He has left an apple-
core upon the table here, next to my journal. I will
attempt to record it for posterity:

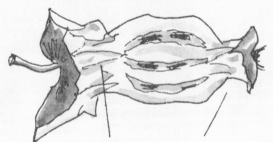

        The Marks of his splendid teeth!
I shall put it under my pillow tonight, & dream of
a Serpentless Eden.

June 6th

   Miss Godwit entreated us to join her & Mr Jelley
in a boating trip upon Slacktrusswater.

   "For", cried Miss G. "I have such a longing to see
Mr Wordsmith's noble brows, reflected in the sparkling
water! To feel myself propelled along, by the manly
strength of his oarsmanship."
At which William smiled modestly.

   Did not feel inclined for a boat trip, myself, my
stomach being uneasy again, but not wishing to spoil
the party, I prepared a picnic of vegetarian dishes.
(Tho' Mr Jelley has not taken more than a few handfulls of meadow-grass, since his arrival. He looks
shockingly pale indeed.) Iris has subjected his ankle
to one of her poultices, which proved beneficial.

      We arrived at the lake at 11 and a beautiful
       morning it was, the towering mass of Wastskull
      Fell reflected in the glassy depths. Wm. rowed
   us out upon the lake, & all exclaimed upon the
beauty of the vista: Cholericke revived from his
torpor & enquired, when we would disembark at
Malta? (v. diverting!)

Menu
for Vegetarian
Picnic

Broom-Rape
Soup

Bastard Toadflax
Bake

Ivy-leaved Sow-
bread

Pimpernel Cutlets

Bindweed
Sandwiches

Thistle Scones

Thistle
Scones
(Called in France,
Pricquembouche)

Miss Godwit looked very beautiful, in her white lappet and dove-grey pelisse, & W^ms eyes sparkled most unnaturally. I felt more than usually sea-sick, but sang the Te Deum to steady my nerves. Iris also sick.

On a sudden, we heard a halloo, & beheld the Leech Pedlar swimming towards us, with a letter strapped to his hat. 'Twas for Mr Jelley — the young man broke the seal with as loud a cry as I have heard.

THE JOLLY BEGGAR

Water Caltrops

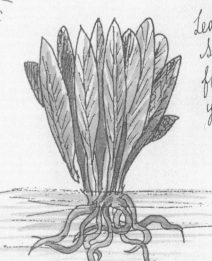

"'Tis from your father, Mary!" he cried. "He knows of our sojourn with the Wordsmiths & is at this moment in hot pursuit, bowling down Clattering Crags in a chase-and-pair. Hark ee.......

    I will take the liberty of attending you at Vole Cottage (he writes) where you will be kind enough to explain, why you have stolen away my daughter, & subjected her to matrimony, a state of which I have the deepest abhorrence, confounding her Feminist Education, etc, etc, — see p. 398 of my book Politicall Justice for further observations on the subject."

Leaves
Sea-Lavender-
flowers not
yet out

I had only
Water-Flowers
at hand: Feverfew
would have dispelled
Mr J's Melancholy

"We cannot return to Vole Cottage!" cried Miss G. "My Papa, when furious, is beyond the reason he pretends to espouse —"

" Can you not convey us to the further shore?" beseeched Mr Jelly. "We could alight there and flee westwards, to Whitehaven perhaps, & there take a boat —"

"To Genoa," suggested Iris, remembering her Italian sailor.

At the thought of Italy, Mr Jelley fainted with pleasure. I insisted that Miss Godwit should take our provisions with her, & guessing at the pair's imprudence, I took out my purse.

"I have 2 guineas here, Miss Godwit " I said ('Twas the Arrowroot money, but no matter.)

"Take it & may Fortune bless you." (Stopped myself only just in time from all mention of Divinity!)

"Dear Dorothy!" cried Cholericke, "Whilst you are in the vein, could I trouble you for five pounds, to assist me in my journey, to the Scottish Highlands? To be repaid, of course, when I launch my magazine — The Wayfarer, will be its name."

"The Sponger, would be more appropriate —

muttered William, for my ears only —
I coughed, to hide his words. W^m made a false
stroke, & lost the oars — the sky grew suddenly
dark, & large spots of rain smacked down upon my
bonnet —

"Alas!" I cried "We are cast adrift, & a storm
threatens! How Fortune can change, from moment
to moment!"

Mr Jelley revived from his swoon, marked the
black clouds, & bared his breast, to the lightning-
flash. Miss Godwit, pale & hectic, clung violently
to William's sleave, ~~I do not know why she~~
~~presumed~~ I was sick; Iris, sicker; Cholericke,
intoxicated by the storm, began to compose aloud-
the Leech Pedlar was carried from our side, by a
great wave, & whirled away into oblivion, the
boat dived & split & with one Universall Cry,
our party was tossd pell-mell upon the
BOSOM of the DEEP!!!

THE JOLLY

Tho' dragged down by my skirts, I was very astonished to feel solid ground beneath my feet, saw trees; waded & plunged, towards them, & gained a pebbly shore, where I was soon joined by dear William, thank Heaven!

The rest of our party was also safe, tho' Mr Jelley & Miss Godwit declined our invitation, to return home & dry themselves: fearing her father's wrath more than a fever, they ran off dripping into the woods, crying ARRIVEDERCI.

W^m watched their departure with a serious brow. I tried to distract him, by pointing out a host of daffodils, growing round the lake, & whipped by the wind, into a kind of dance, but in vain.

Walked home v. miserable & wet thro' to the skin. W^m silently brooding, C. singing snatches of old songs, Iris complaining, myself v. weary & ill.

"Daffodil," remarked William on a sudden, "now that would be a very pleasant name, for a GIRL."

This odd remark stuck in my mind somehow, & discomposed me v. much.

Wᵐ Godwit, Philosopher & Enraged Parent

Arrived home to find a chaise-and-pair in the lane. At our approach, a small gentleman, wearing spectacles and with a massive brow, leapt out.

It was William Godwit, Mary's Enraged Parent. He greeted us with great courtesy, tho' was short-sighted enough, to address Iris as Miss Wordsmith —whereat Wᵐ cried—

"That is not my sister, that is the maid!"

"I beg your pardon Ma'am", said Mr Godwit, turning to the Portugal Laurel bush, "my sight is dim", and he bowed low to the astonished tree!

"This is my sister, sir!" cried William, thrusting me forward.

"A thousand pardons, Ma'am!" said Mr G. "I took you for a port!"

Offered Mr G. a glass of cordial, which he accepted. Mercifully. he would not linger, but set off in pursuit of the unlucky lovers. W^m however, directed him East, towards Newcastle, whence he assured Mr G. they were to embark for Norway. I cannot but hope that, with such mis-direction & such poor eyesight, he is unlikely to intercept his errant child.

Vole Cottage.

ITALY

There were several pools of water, upon the flag-stones from our wet clothes. Iris immediately set about them, whilst W^m & Cholericke steamed by the fire (especially Cholericke) discussing The Imagination. I withdrew into the pantry, where I changed into a dry shift. Alas! The remains of the Sago-Pudden crashed down upon my head. This proved the last straw, and I retired v. ill, to the linen cupboard, & slept curled up there, for some fifteen hours. (Cholericke sleeps in my room, now the Jelleys are gone)

June 7th .... All v. ill! agues, etc. Slept, & read the Faerie Queen.

June 8th The departure of the Jelleys seems to have cleared away some dark clouds from my mind, and W^m & Cholericke having embarked upon a long excursion to the Nattering Naws (which will necessitate their absence for 2 days) Iris & I set about re-covering the bolsters & mattress with new ticking.

The Sun Peeping in at my window 8 June

I spied a flea upon W^{ms} mattress - much mortified thereat, but Iris despatched it, with a ~~skilfull thum~~ skillful thumb-nail. The sight of W^{ms} blood, upon Iris's nail, made a v. curious impression on my Fancy.

The Leech-Pedlar brought a letter from my dear friend Mary Hitchinson, who tells me that the Yellow Weasel's Snout is blooming in Yorkshire, & here its leaves are scarce peeping forth. What a difference, between the steaming tropical South, & our wild & savage North-Country! Yet I own I would not change places with dear Mary, for anything. She has her Yellow Weasel's Snout, but I have my Beloved William.

June 9th   Second day of W^m & Cholericke's absence. By now they must have ascended The Nattering Naws. Providence protect them from any damage from the granite pinnacles!

To Starch ...... 6^d
To Agar. Agar.... 3/4^d

W^{ms} Blood
upon Iris's
Finger.

The Flee

June 10th

Two letters came for Cholericke – both tear stained. ~~I gazed at them~~ Both in a lady's hand, but different hands (I mean of course, different ladies!) (Much diverted at this thought!) I gazed at them awhile, wondering what their contents were, and feeling v. sad that poor Cholericke's heart should be so divided. Feel he was not entirely _sound_ in his choice of a wife. Had his choice been less fanciful… had he, instead, taken to wife an old friend, perhaps— I own I shed a tear at my sad reflections. But I myself am the happiest of women. ~~Sometimes I think I love William best, & sometimes Cholericke.~~

CHOLERICKE
DOROTHY

3 × 36 = er

CHOLERICKE
DOROTHY

June 11th

Wm & Cholericke still not returned. Some alarm has crept into my soul at their continued absence. Suppose they have tumbled down a scree, & lie twisted & broken in a gully, lashed by this bitter wind!

Idle stuff!

To Soda 1½d

Wind so strong, it blew down the chimney & whipped the crust off a fine plumb-pie I had baked.

St. Walter's Day (12th June)

SUET PUDDEN
12 oz of Flour
6 oz of ~~Boulders~~
    Suet
1 teaspoonful of
~~Blood~~ Baking-Powder
¼ teaspoon Salt
Cold Water

METHOD
Mix the dry
ingredients &
then add water
until a ~~crevasse~~
appears stiff
paste is formed.
Shape it into
a roll, & wrap in
a ~~mist~~ pudding-
cloth — Put in
Boiling Water
& cook for 2¼
~~days~~ hours.
The above mixture
may also be made
into ~~Jumblings~~
Dumplings.

Still no sign of W^m & C. Am almost frantic with worry — running to the door every five minutes, & peering down the lane. Iris tried to soothe my jangling nerves, by the offer of a herbal tea, but I threw it on the fire, in my agitation. I am attempting to distract myself ~~by~~ from all thoughts of disaster, by reading <u>Titus Andronicus</u>.

If only my darlings are restored to me without injury, what a life of blissful peace & retirement we will lead! With only the wind in the trees and the song of the Pratincole to disturb the deep throb of scholarship & contemplation, & no trivial intrusions, nor, one hopes, unwanted guests, to distract poor W^m from his work.

Made a dismal & solitary supper of suet-pudden and buttermilk. Was sick, & went to bed early, but could not sleep, so at 2 am. crept into William's bed, & slumbered at last there with a pair of his stockens wrapped around my head, for comfort — Wind still v. strong — Mrs G's poke bonnet, blown to Ambleside.

June 13th

Day of wind and rain — A great crowd of slugs
hurled against the window pane. Nothing like it known
before, and the little Ragged Boy called to say he had
seen, up on the Jabbercock Rock, the ghost of Old
Sankey — a fearful figure apparently, with the body
of a man, an eagle's head, and the ——— of a babboon.
To glimpse old Sankey, said the boy is a sure sign
of a violent death in the vicinity.

When he told me this, I bit quite through my little
finger, but Iris stitched the tip back on with twine,
and we have hopes it may knit. But what is the loss
of a fingertip compared with the loss of a Dearest
Brother and Friend?

I see them now, lying stark and ghastly beneath a pile of fallen boulders, their pat

Oh! They are COME HOME!
I hear Wm's step

June 14th

Wm & Cholericke returned last night at 7pm, just as I was writing my Journal, muddy but triumphant – having walked 200 miles and composed some glorious lyrics. So glad.

Now we can settle to our life of peaceful work and the contemplation, of Universal Truths.

June 15th

A bad night. Awoken by hystericall screaming from below: my first thought was that an intruder had surprised Iris beneath the mangle, and was now making an attempt either on her virtue or her life. Seizing my chamberpot, I ran downstairs, thinking to crack it upon the skull of her assailant – but the scullery was empty, & more screams from the parlour, identified the sufferer as poor Cholericke, caught in the toils of night-mare.

"God help me, there is an aardvark loose in my breeches!" he cried, as we shook him awake. He continued to weep above ten minutes, at the memory of his dream.

them, not me!!

"'Tis the rain," he explained. "Wind, and rainy-weather, affect me in the most fatal manner: sweats, winds, & griping ~~diarear~~ ~~diario~~ diarrhoea are my destiny, I'm sure, unless I remove to the <u>Mediterranean</u>!"

Whereat he ran off to the Necessary, Iris following with a sprig of Viola Tricolor (known locally as <u>Jump Up & Kiss Me</u>). She declared it would disperse the qualm, if C. were so bold as to thrust it into his nostrils.

Whilst C. was absent I changed his sheets — they were quite drenched with sweat.

"Poor soul!" I cried, "How he does suffer!" William snorted, at which I was much surprised.

"Half Cholericke's ills," he muttered, "are naught but <u>Imagination</u> — there are those, even under this roof, Dorothy, who suffer ten times more than he has ever done, but in silence — and what consolation do they receive?"

So saying, he went abruptly upstairs, taking the candle and leaving me in the dark, & wracked with guilt & consternation, I burst into tears.

I crept to William's door, & asked if he was ill.

Viola
Tricolor

Iris's Remedy
for a
Ganglion

Strike the ganglion,
quite unexpectedly,
with a cast-iron
candlestick
at midnight

Ganglion

"Look here!" he said, in an undertone, throwing back the sheet, "Pray tell me, Dorothy — is that not a ganglion?"

I could not say for certain what it was, never having seen such a thing before, but I rather thought it to be one of his lower ribs, thrown into unusual relief, by the candlelight.

"The exquisite agony and suffocation of breathing which I endure as the result of this ganglion upon my right lung," whispered William, "no one will ever know, for I suffer in silence."

He spoke between clenched teeth, & his breathing was heavy: I sponged his brow, & stroked his hand, until he fell asleep, then hastened down-stairs & did the same for poor Cholericke.

Once he slept, I returned to my own bed, but since only an hour was left of the night before we I had to rise, & bake bread, I read the first three acts of King John, & many a tear I shed.

June 16th

V. tired this day. On Iris's advice, Cholericke
spent the day with pansies & violets peeping from
each nostril.

"I have a nose-gay!" he quipped, which diverted
me very much, but it seemed to irritate poor Wm,
who walked alone up to the Shivering Riggs. C. & I
walked down to the Nattering Bottoms. An old man
passed us on the road, stared at C's nostrils & cried

"And from thy fair & unpolluted flesh
    May violets spring!"

Then he vanished, into a copse of alders. Astonishing!
I took him for a wandering scholar, but C. very
disturbed, said it was a ~~propecty~~ prophesy of his
early death, & that we should go home straight-
way, as he did not wish to die upon the road.

"A great weakness," he cried, "has seized my
Bowels: my ankles buckle, my heart flutters, like a
caged bird: sweat bursts from my Brows, ~~like~~ as
from the Steaming Geysers of Iceland, Dorothy.

—I am sinking, sinking, sinking!"—

Cholericke's
Nose-Gay

And he dropt to his knees in a flooded wheel-rut.

The view from Nattering Bottoms was so fine, however, that it reviv'd him: we could see up to the very top of Shivering Riggs.

I noticed a tiny figure up there, scrambling towards the summit, & recognised it as William, by the darns in his great coat. C. not convinced, said it was an aardvaark. C. rather confused.

At home, C. collapsed in a stupher upon the sopa — I mean a stupor upon the sopha. W^m & I walked in the orchard, & resolved to encourage poor dear Cholericke to undertake his long-postponed trip to Scotland: W^m going so far as to say that, to finance Cholerick's departure, he was willing to sell Great Aunt Judith's long-case clock. Good gracious! But I know what he means.

June 17th

Beautiful mild day. Good King Henry is crowding out the carrots. W^m wrote The Ganglion.

Dear Clock!
But still . . . . .

Rook Pie

6 Young Rooks,
¾ lb Rumpsteak
½ pt Stock,
Paste —
  Skin the rooks
without plucking
them by cutting
the skin near
the thighs, &
drawing it over
the body & head.
Split —
Oh. I feel
a little faint.

June 18th

Another lovely day: low-hanging clouds of the mildest grey.

Cholericke quite restored to health and amiable manners. V. affectionate towards us, & could not speak too highly of William's Ganglion.

All the same, Wm asked Mr Northeby to call, & value the clock.

I made a rook pie.

June 19th   A fox broke into the wash-house last night, scattering Mr Pickerell's sketches & notes. Mr Pickerell surprised it, & in a rage, killed it by stabbing it through the heart, with a 2B drawing pencil. Iris is preparing a Fox Pâté from the innards, & Mrs Grindstone has offered to stuff & mount the creature for us.

"When it comes to stuffin' and mountin'," she observed, "there was nobody to touch me owd Jeremiah: he were an artist!" We took this to be a reference to her late husband.

June 20th

St Gertrude's Day. Today W^m dunged the
lettuce-patch, & I sowed the scarlet beans (too
late really, alas! But have been v. distracted!) The
weeds thrust up everywhere — and a for the slugs—
I am in despair — nor can I account for their
existence in a benign universe.

William's method with them is to go out into the
garden, by candle-light, impale them upon an old
pen, and fling them over the house & into the lane.

This evening, alas, Mrs Grindstone happened to
be passing, & I fancy, by the exclamation she
made, that she sustained a wounded slug, upon
her poke-bonnet.

June 21st — A letter from solicitors, in Weather-
by, telling us of a remote Uncle of ours, who has
dyed, leaving us £80 !!! Spent the day in fantastical
dreaming. W^m declares, he will have an Ovid and
a new Paradise Lost; I would be grateful for glass-
windows in my bed-room, I admit. Cholericke
revolves plans for us all to visit Katmandu !

June 22nd

William & Cholericke perusing maps of the
East-Indies: I celebrated our new wealth by
carrying some coales, & some old tea-leaves, to Mrs
Grindstone. She greeted me with a surly nod—
"I see your Old Man's Beard has got The Wilt",
she remarked — this news astounded me. She must
have meant my clematis, my pride & joy, the one
named Mrs Cholmeley.

I ran home all anxiety, & twas true: all the
flower-buds and leaf buds hanging their heads
and the whole plant a picture of shame & sorrow.
I tried what a little starch would do, but in vain.
Cried, & sang Mozart's Requiem. (Wm dislikes Mozart,
finds him too modern & depraved a taste, but I
am secretly taken, & sing his scores to myself
in bed — silently, of course.)

June 23rd   I write this in a snatched ten
minutes before we leave for our Scottish journey.
(Katmandu, & the East Indies, are postponed until
next year.) So much to do: packing clothes, food, etc-

To Pack

Wm's stockens
Wm's _____s
Wm's flannel vests
Wm's breeches
Wm's corduroy
mountain-breeches
Wm's leather
   waistcoat
Wm's woollen
   caps
Wm's fell-trousers
Wm's greatcoat
Wm's cotton shirts
Wm's garters
Wm's braces
Wm's handkerchiefs
Wm's spare bootlaces.
Wm's knife
Wm's pens
Wm's pencils
Wm's paper + ink
My Cloak
My Walking stick

looking to the garden, giving Iris precise instructions (she is to be left in charge, as Mr Pickerell, is to follow us upon our journey, at a discreet distance, sketching the beauties of nature.) I hope in our absence Iris will not be tempted into over-familiarity with anyone. (I have asked Mrs Grindstone to keep an eye upon her.)

June 24th   All is ready. We have, upon Cholericke's advice, hired a small jaunting car, such as the Irish use. Our first impulse was to walk, but upon further consideration of William's ganglion, Cholericke's Diarrhoea, & my headaches, we felt a small cart might prove its worth.

I fear it may restrict us to the valley-roads, however, away from the upland paths which have so delighted dear William (like an eagle, he soars to the rocks!)

June 25th   We have today completed less than 30 miles — much less, as C. remarked, than he could have accomplished on foot. The reason was, some obstruction in the jaunting-car made the wheels stick badly, whenever it rained —

The TOAD
& EARWIG

which, alas, it often did. Several times we were obliged to get out and push, to assist the labours of the poor horse, who seems v. ill & thin.

We have put up at The Toad & Earwig, at Kirby-Hawkington and hope to arrive at Gretna-Green tomorrow night, where I hope we will secure a better inn than we have found here.

William is gone forth to seek the services of a wheelwright, Cholericke to see a local waterfall known as Cold Dash Falls.

I prevailed upon our hostess (a slatternly woman, who made no distinction between her apron & her handkerchief) to furnish us with a fire, & by its pitiful flicker (but 2 birch-twigs & a mossy log) I am attempting to dry our clothes, for we got soaked to the skin, today, several times.

We supped upon a great Egg, fried in stale Pig's Lard (I was reminded of Lord Byro, & felt a PANG) The Mistress of the House said 'twas a Turkey's Egg, but Cholericke declared it, a Dodo's. To bed. Damp sheets, & lichen on the bedknobs. To Inn... 3d

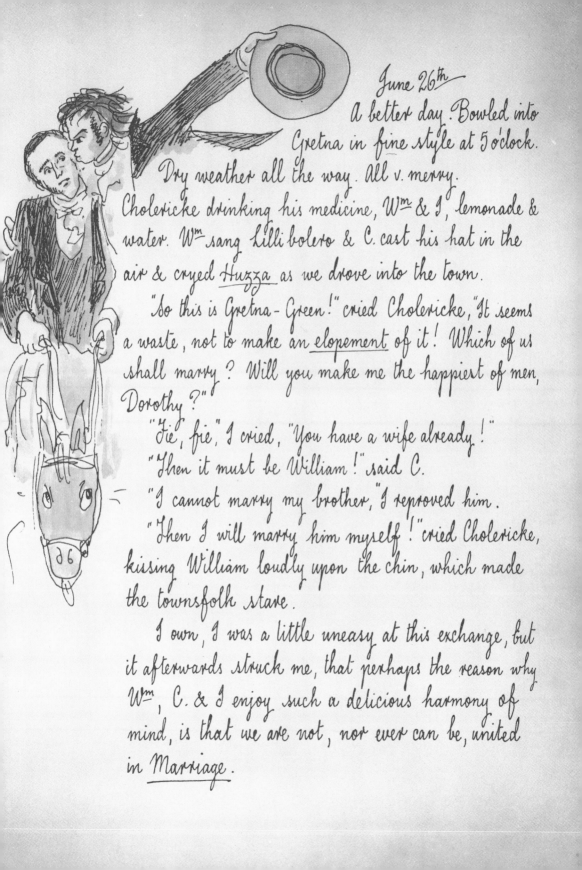

June 26th

A better day. Bowled into Gretna in fine style at 5 o'clock. Dry weather all the way. All v. merry. Cholericke drinking his medicine, Wᵐ & I, lemonade & water. Wᵐ sang Lilli bolero & C. cast his hat in the air & cryed _Huzza_ as we drove into the town.

"So this is Gretna-Green!" cried Cholericke, "It seems a waste, not to make an _elopement_ of it! Which of us shall marry? Will you make me the happiest of men, Dorothy?"

"Fie, fie," I cried, "You have a wife already!"

"Then it must be William!" said C.

"I cannot marry my brother," I reproved him.

"Then I will marry him myself!" cried Cholericke, kissing William loudly upon the chin, which made the townsfolk stare.

I own, I was a little uneasy at this exchange, but it afterwards struck me, that perhaps the reason why Wᵐ, C. & I enjoy such a delicious harmony of mind, is that we are not, nor ever can be, united in _Marriage_.

We lay upon the village-green in the evening sunshine, spying on the clandestine couples as they strolled arm in arm on the grass. And a very pretty sight they made. I own I shed a tear ~~at some thoughts of~~

The Ruined Abbey.

June 27th

Our wheels & spirits mended, we set out upon the main-road to Glasgow, (a 3 days' journey) which we must pass, before the Highland Beauties unfold. We dined at Ecclenackie upon a bacon rasher so thick & hairy, I felt we were addressing ourselves to a Broyled Doormat.

The incessant jolting of the jaunting-car, the glare of the open road, & the horrors of digestion, conspired towards a v. bad headache.

The rest of this & the next day I spent with my eyes closed, tho' the sounds of W. & C. arguing, about Resolution & Independence, penetrated my conciousness.

What a wondrous thing is the Masculine Organ of Speculation! Would that I were so blest!

To inn 7½ᵈ.   To headachepowder ¾ᵈ

Oh! I think I am getting one of my migraines!

June 30th — (I think.)

At last my Headache began to mend, as we drove
into Glasgow, where we collected letters from the Post
Office.   One from my dear Mary Hitchinson,
who tells me that her NOTHOLIRION MACROPHYLLUM,
has got the Black Rot. I am not surprised. If only
she would confine herself to our native plants! Why,
Gorse, Heather & Thistle are handsome enough,
are they not?

Cholericke made a mysterious trip into a strange
street, near the docks, — something to do with his
little brown bottle, I am sure. (The horse consumed
the last of it, yesterday.)

He returned disappointed, his cloak drawn around
him, & with a shaking-fit.

"'Tis the humid stench of the Clyde," he said,

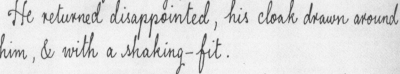

"I fear, the return of my diarrhoea! I should have gone to Sicily — Byro advised it — wet, & windy weather, are fatall to my bowells."

W^m gave him a peppermint, & he was quiet for a while.

We lodged at the Paisley Arms, a large commercial place. Several manufactures are being set up at the water-side, & the smokes & the sounds of their engines, seem like a glimpse of hell.

In the darkest void of the night, a piercing scream, and feverish panting, announced another of poor Cholericke's nightmares. Our host arrived with a candle: we shook the dreamer awake, & he seized W^{m's} hand, wild eyed & drenched in sweat.

"Good G——!" he cried, "Mercy on us! My dear friends! I dreamt, I was a Pickled Gherkin!! The ancient Beldame, Fortune, was about to feast on me! I was impaled upon her fork! She raised me to her scabby lips!"

Here he broke off, & endured a series of the most heart-vending shudders.

Cholericke's Dream

"Our friend is often vexed with dreams," I explained to the Landlord, who, relieved there was no _crime_ committed beneath his roof, retired to his bed. I stroked C's poor brow until he fell asleep.

This made me think, that it is many weeks since dear William confided his dreams to me: I questioned him about it, at breakfast, but he only shrugged and said, he had had none lately.

He avoided my eye, however — a thing he seldom does. Misgivings seethe in my bosom.

To inn, 6ᵈ.

July 1ˢᵗ — soon left behind the smokes & night-mares of Glasgow; northwards, & feasted our eyes upon green fields & lovely moors.

My heart danced, & Wᵐ smiled. C. still v. ill, shivering in his cloak; we had to stop for him several times, & his groans, behind the rocks & trees were quite terrible to hear — reminding me, in a way, of the alarm-call of the Great Bustard.

There was no inn at Cailliemagrachan, so we lodged at a modest cottage, by the road-side.

Part of a
scottish Castle!

(Wᵐ says, he
prefers Natures
pinnacles, to
Man's!)

Our hosts, a carpenter & his wife, had seven child-
ren. Their kitchen was also home to a fair large sow,
a goose, & a cockerell; but they offered us a straw
pallet, on which we slept all 3, kept warm by a
rug of wolf's skin, & by the mingled heat of our
bodies (especially Cholericke's — W^m tends, at night,
to go cold & numb, in his extremities.) I, lying between
them, was too excited by the novelty of our situation,
to close my eyes all night. But I watched the embers
glow, the cockerell twitch upon its perch, & heard
the pig snore, with a curious sense of delight.

We made a good breakfast upon oatmeal & water.
The bairns all looked v. sturdy, & our hostess, tho'
clearly with child again, contrived her household
duties with such thoroughness, as to polish the
the pig in the morning, burning its dung upon
the fire, & finding time to be pleasant with its
tail.   Gave her 3^d, on leaving. W^m said it was
far too much, but I felt sure I was right (Also
feel sure about Mozart, but never mind.)

Country
Comforts!

June 2nd

V. tired, & slept upon the road, as the cart clattered along. Awoke to see purple mountains, wild water-falls, gorse, heather, eagles wheeling in the blue vault of heaven: in short,

The Highlands!

So ravished by the sight, I burst into tears directly! William & C. also in tears. We cried by the road side a good half hour, then William proposed, that I should drive on in the cart alone, whilst he & Cholericke climbed The Rumbling Lassie (a formid-able peak, its sides covered with treacherous scree.)

I obeyed, tho' imagining a wolf at my neck at every bend in the road — which alternated in my mind, with ideas of Wm & dear C. suffocated beneath a fall of scree. But I arrived at Inverillock unmauled by wolves, & secured rooms at The Auld Snookey — the only inn, & little more than a hen-house. Black-ned beams, blackened ceilings: an infernall darkness prevailed, & the smell quite revolting. I thought of dear Vole Cottage, and shed many a tear.

Eagles.
(Wm swears they were Buzzards)

Dr Wm's Boot! ↑

My bed, was quite crawling with vermin: <u>I could see it move</u>. I asked for food, & walked up & down: presently a small boy entered with a foul old crumpet which time had brought, to the condition of OOLITIC LIMESTONE.

Fearing the infestation of the bed, & lacking chairs or rugs, I stretched myself out upon the mantelpiece, securing myself by means of a few rusty hooks, to the ceiling. Attached by my stays & bootstraps,

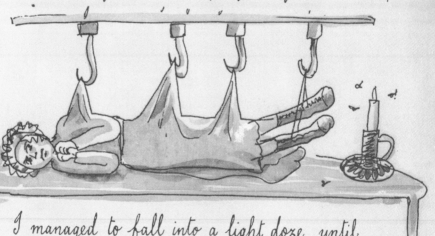

I managed to fall into a light doze, until Williams familiar rap startled me from a dream of gooseberry - tart, & a roaring fire. No breakfast, & the ~~tot~~ reckoning 3½ᵈ, which C. declared, the ~~Host~~ should pay his Guests, for inflicting upon them the almost ingenious discomforts of the place.

July 3rd

The day fine : but an old man, we met upon the road remarked that the ~~days~~ *nights* are drawing in.

Feeling v. hungry, after 2 hours' drive, we saw in a nearby field, a highland cow of magnificent size, and shaggy coat. Could we obtain some milk, we wondered? W^m declared himself unsuited for the errand, his person being strangely abhorrent to the animal kingdom (we have often noticed this) I was too afraid to approach the beast.

Cholericke, scorning us both for cowards, approached the creature and grabbed its udder — alas! 'Twas a Bull- its long hair, had concealed the Truth, and poor C. was tossed over the hedge — his breeches quite in tatters.

"Patch away, Patchaway, Dorothy," he cried, pulling off what remained of them, "They are my only pair, & I'm determined, they shall last me till Michaelmas —"

Luckily I had brought my needle, but lacking thread, I darned up C.'s breeches, with rye grass, whilst C. hid ~~beneath~~ behind a hawthorn - hedge.

Highland-
Cattle
alas! My Cows are always so Inadequate!

A Pittock's Nest in a Pine Tree. (Eggs, Cold)

The Pittock (a bad parent)

"Like Odysseus," he remarked, "when he met Nausicaa, after his shipwreck, upon the shore." William seemed impatient, and strode off up Ben Na Craignach, whilst I stitched & C. lurked.

Back on the road, all faint with hunger. I spied a Pittock's nest, high in a pine-tree, & climbed it, despite petticoats. (Wᵐ & C. deep in debate about Fortitude.) Found the eggs cold, so the theft only a theft, not murder, & brought them safely down, in the crown of my bonnet. We sucked them raw, tho' Cholevicke's was embryonick. (He declared this was a omen.)

After ~~dinner~~ this, we made a v. weary climb, across a great gaunt pass — at the summit of which, we leapt out to admire a marvellous panorama. Wᵐ declared he could see as far as Auchterargie, & I certainly certainly spied, some 150 miles distant, a sailing-ship — from the crew's uniforms, concluded it to be a Norwegian vessell.

Whilst we were gazing upon the vista, heard a groan and strange crumpling sound behind us.

Turned round, to find our horse had collapsed, poor creature! Held its head and sang the Te Deum to it: it expired in my arms & my tears rained down its mane.

"Let us feast upon it!" cried Cholericke (an idea, which shocked me very much) But so great was our hunger, that our poor horse was not decently cold, but three large rump - steaks were sizzling upon a peat fire W^m had contrived.

My sentiments and stomach debated the issue: nearly fainting with hunger, I found the sizzling, and the smell, too delicious to resist, and devoured my erstwhile friend, like a ravening wolf.

After this meal, we felt our strength returning to our veins. But the danger of our situation began now to awaken our fears — we were horseless, stranded upon a remote mountain top, our possessions in the cart, the cart useless without the horse.

"If one of us was prepared to stand between the shafts, and bear the harness on his back," said Cholericke, "Then we could roll downhill, to the Dounes of Muckart, & get a new horse, there."

A Highland Lament.

A Horse
since thou hast
Perforce
Given up
the ghost
We were
O, forced!
to eat
thy Corse
Roarst

not quite
Right

6

"I cannot oblige you," frowned William. "The position of my ganglion, would make any contact with a harness, unendurable."

"You must not risk your health, William!" I cried, "Perhaps dear Cholericke will perform the office."

"Alas" said Cholericke, sniffing the air, "I smell rain, my friends — rain brings on diarrhoea — my Flying Gout is rising — I can feel it, this moment — ascending to my clavicles — the issue will be desperate —"

"I shall draw us, then!" I cried, and though they protested, I tucked up my petticoats, wriggled into the harness, and seized the shafts of the cart.

"Bravo, Dorothy!" cried Cholericke, and William cracked the reins playfully across my shoulders, as we resumed our journey.

"There will be no need for exertion on your part, Dorothy!" cried William, "'Tis all downhill from here to the Downes of Muckart!"

Alas, however! The brakes were broken, the cart bowled

along at a furious rate, and I was forced to gallop in a kind of frenzy; my bonnet flew off, my petticoat was torn to shreds, my boots burst — I am sure, that we fled downhill at no less, than 25 miles an hour, until we arrived at the Dounes of Muckart—

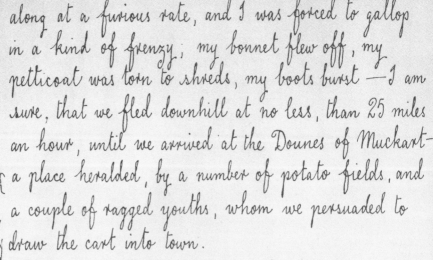

Dounes of Muckart

The Muck

a place heralded, by a number of potato fields, and a couple of ragged youths, whom we persuaded to draw the cart into town.

I crawled back to my place beside William, who had driven me the seven miles with great skill.

"Not bad going, Dorothy," said he, "but we shall have to get you re-shod, I fear."

I could not help laughing at this pleasantry of his.

A Deer

Wᵐ says 'tis like a cat on stilts!

"..... and you held the shafts a little too low for perfect balance, my dear."

I was sad, to have disappointed my beloved Brother, in this particular.

We lodged with a Mrs Mac Muckartie, a most surprising woman. She had lived at Leyden, in the Netherlands, (married a Dutch-man, she had met at Earlsferry Harbour, where she used to sell pickled pike.) Her husband, a Minheer Julius Onzerleeveheerbeestje, had given her six sons, & died of <u>algae</u>. Her six sons were now sailing the Seven Seas (one sea each and one to share—as she pleasantly put it.)

She had returned to her native Dounes to die, but instead, married an old sweetheart, Angus MacMuckartie, & returned to her old trade of pickled-fish.

She lived in a neat cottage by the bridge over the Muck, & she set before us a most acceptable meal of pickled gurnard, & spiced biscuits, called in Dutch "Speculaas."

"I wonder," cried Cholericke, "if they will assist <u>Speculation</u>?"

Slept v. well on a straw pallet in Mrs McM's attic: Wᵐ & C. slept in her barn, where the pickled fish hung on wooden racks. All scrupulously clean, but they did not escape a

Mrs MacMuckartie's Recipe for Pickled Gurnard

Gut the Gurnard, reserving the gall-bladder.
Seeth it in a quart of ripe rainwater, till the gills flap.
Take a scalded jar (use a cloth!) add a squeeze of gall-bladder.
Strain the gurnard, & assist it into the jar. Pour over a pint of whisky-vinegar & seal.
© Mrs MacMuckartie.

slight odour.

July 5th — Mrs Mac Muckartie rose at 5, and scrubbed the road outside her door.

We breakfasted upon pickled eel (the way W^m snapt their heads off, was very stylish) and set out in excellent spirits.

A new horse, young and well-fed, kept up a brisk trot, & the great beech trees along our way shone with a beautiful gleam. My heart seemed to swell with joy, and with dear Cholericke's head upon my shoulder, & mine upon W^m's, I felt the most exquisite sensation of peace and harmony.

As we bowled along, a bird flew out of the bracken, gave a strange cry, and winged its way into a distant tree.

"What was that?" I cried.

"A Dotterel", replied W^m. — "No, no, W^m," asserted C. "'Twas an Aberfeldy Snipe, I saw its ridged wing bars".

"'Twas a Dotterel", affirmed W^m.

"Come, come, W^m," said C. "What do you know of the

Perforated St Johns Wort. (I must admit, I did not know St John had been perforated. Poor soul! Christianity is so full of examples of Man's Inhumanity. Alas!)

<u>Linnaean genera</u> ? 'Twas a Snipe."

"As to the <u>Linnaean genera</u>," cried William, "What do you know of my familiarity with it ? I have studied deeply of this subject, Cholericke – from books, & from my own Observation. 'Twas a ~~A~~ Dotterel."

"'Twas a Snipe!" cried Cholericke, flinging off his cloak in exasperation.

"Devil take you! 'Twas a Dotterel!"

"Pray have a care, W^m !" I cried, "Drive more slowly! You will overturn us!"

William turned to me with a stern look.

"You, Dorothy, must settle the question for us – was it a Dotterel, or a Snipe?"

"I am not entirely sure," I faltered, "but I rather supposed it to be a kind of Great Skobby."

"A Skobby! What nonsense you talk!" cried W^m — at which I could not restrain a tear.

"You are too severe on Dorothy!" cried Cholericke,

seizing my hand.

"No, No!" I cried (for he felt clammy again, & I was sure he was not well.) "William is as severe as he pleases — I am sure, I am quite happy—"

"Always so patient under rebuke, dear Dorothy!" Cholericke pressed my hand to his lips—"You should rise up against this tyranny, my dear."

"Tyranny!" cried William, "How dare you!"

"Yes sir, tyranny!" cried C. "If you dislike my words, stop the cart & let's settle this, with blows!"

"Oh no, my darlings!" I screamed, but in vain. William reined the horse, & the stillness, as the cart stopped, seemed palpitating — only the sound of the wind in the trees as W. & C. glared at each other.

"You exploit your poor sister!" cried C. "beyond endurance! Her only care is for your comfort— I have never seen an existence more dedicated to slavery!"

"Hush, Cholericke!" I pleaded.

"What can you say of female exploitation?" thundered William, standing up, with the whip.

Pinis
Sylvestris
(Scotch Fir)

(I think Pinis
is not quite right
— am I confusing it
with something
else?)

"Where is your wife? When does she ever see you? Would your bairns recognise their father? You are the pattern, Cholericke, of domestick irresponsibility—"

"Make sport with my misfortune!" cried C. "I see it is your way. I had thought, you were sympathetic to my miseries."

"I am sick of your miseries!" cried W^m "Damn your Diarrhoea! A plague on your Secret Loves!"

"And what of your <u>Secret Love</u>?" hissed C, at which my heart bounded in terror.

"Speak not of what you are ignorant!" cried William.

"Descend yourself!" cried C—"I will drive on, with Dorothy, & rescue her from her <u>bondage</u>."

"I do not wish, dear Cholericke, to be rescued from anything—" I wept.

"As for the money you owe us—" roared W^m

"A gentleman would not have mentioned such a thing!" cried Cholericke "You strike me to the heart!" And he leapt out of the cart & fell into a ditch—as if insensible.

"I resign your debts!" cried W^m "I want no repayment. 'Twas money thrown away, upon addiction and

The Brig
O'Clashie

profligacy."

"Profligacy!" screamed Cholericke, springing to his feet. "How can you accuse me of that? My habits are the most <u>austere</u> — I do not even take tea!"

"We know to well, what you take"— said W^m, looking v. severe.— to the detriment ~~of up~~ not only of your <u>life</u>, but your <u>art</u>.—"

"What do you know of Life, or Art?" roared Cholericke. "Does anything like blood flow in your veins? Has love e'er wracked your soul? What can we say of a poet, who bends his thoughts upon a <u>Withered Turnip</u>?"

"And what of your work?" returned W^m, "Mind-polluting dreams, and romances! <u>Miasma</u> and Hallucination!"

"Oh William!" I cried, clinging to his arm, "Say no more, I beg."

The Tarot's
Warning.

"We shall go, Dorothy", W^m conceded, breathing hard. "This altercation has inflamed my ganglion." He snapt the reins, and off we went, leaving.

Cholericke standing in the lane, & a v. pathetic
figure he made, goose-grass sticking to his hat.
My heart smote me. I cried all the way to
Aberkirklochry. William said nothing, but looked
v. severe.

At Aberkirklochry we dined in silence at a road-
side hotel, upon a strange bird, not v. well plucked,
and hardly cooked. William poked at it with his fork—
"It is a Dotterel"— said he, with satisfaction,
and consumed the whole.

I was so depressed in spirits, I had no
appetite for anything but a few damp feathers.
After dinner, Wm walked, & I sat by a stream,
making daisy chains & gazing at the rattling
water, as if hypnotised, & thought of poor Ophelia's
tragic end, as I wound the daisies around my neck.

Wm returned; said his mind was eased.
"Sixteen miles of steep granite, can have a marvellously
comforting effect, Dorothy!"

It is signed R.B.
What can it mean?
It is indecent SIC

I found the
following verses
scratched on the
window of our Inn:

Comin' thro' the rye, my jo
& Comin' thro' the rye
She fand a staun o'staunin' graith
Comin' thro' the rye

And we drove on, to The Spittall of Dungmuir. Our Inn was the Knockandhu Arms, a miserable enough place; its sole attendant, a drunk & almost incoherent old man.

We asked for rooms. He spat, but in quite a friendly way, & said something like

"Ye hae garmae fra till hogsarewillie."

(I think we have come too far north.)

He then Showd us a room, with two low beds in it, supposing us married — but it seemed the only room to be had, so we accepted it. Very weary, especially in spirits (since the argument with C. I feel quite stung to the soul.)

"There can be no impropriety", said I. "If we take it in turns to lie fully dressed upon a bed — different beds, I mean, dearest —" I blushed, & faltered — "whilst the other takes the air."

"True, Dorothy", said William, flinging himself upon the larger bed — "my walk has tired me somewhat — I will take the first nap, if you will be so good as to draw off my boots before you go."

Joyfully I executed my dear brother's command, and then descended. The smell of the parlour was so intolerable, I went out & sat on some rocks V. low in spirits, & as time went on, almost starved.

My hunger drove me back to the Knockandhu Arms, where I knocked, timidly enough, at the kitchen door, to enquire for food. There was no answer, but a snore. I peered within. The old man was lying quite stupified, a bottle of whisky in his hand. I tiptoed in, thinking to take a crust, but had the misfortune to tread upon the tail of a great mastiff, who fastened his savage teeth upon my cuff. I struggled to escape, my dress tore, & I fled, leaving the beast devouring my sleeve, his owner still unconscious.

I escaped to the sweet fields, & luckily remembering some of Iris's lore, I found several clumps of a most nourishing herb: Ransoms, or wild garlic,

The Mastiff
One of God's creatures?

NO.
Corrupted by Man
Wm

of which I ate great handfulls and made a delicious dessert upon the white lips of the Dead Nettle, where the most nectar is.

W^m did not awake from his nap, so I spent the night beneath a wet boulder.

July 27th. Have not written in my diary for many days. W^m & I travelled thro' Ballingowrie, Benorchy and Invernethy.

Scenery wild, grand, & lonely. W^m climbed many peaks, including Ben Gussie and Aucht-O'Monachie — but I sat stupified in the cart. The sight of C.'s little leather bag, containing his notebooks & scarf, still tucked under the seat, so mortified me, that I was unable to take much pleasure, even in dear W^{m's} company.

Then at Cracknacruitie as we sat together upon an Alder-bank, throwing twigs idly into the Mallachy, I burst out.

"Dear W^m!" I cried, "I cannot forebear thinking

O Poignant Bag !

S.T.C

about poor Cholericke. To part with him in such bitterness! After so many years of devoted love! Was not he the first man to proclaim your genius? Has he not called down blessings on your head a thousand times? Suffered with us, the blows of fortune? Romped with us upon the Somerset turf? Is he not, despite his unfortunate weakness, the most generous, loving and imaginative of human creatures? My heart breaks, at the thought of our estrangement."

William picked his teeth with an alder twig.

"There is something in what you say, Dorothy", he conceded—"at which my heart bounded—"and yet, I ask you to consider:

Does not Cholericke abuse his body & mind with noxious stimulants?

Does he not, under their ~~stimulant~~ influence, behave with immodesty at times?

Is he not half in love with his own ill-health? (you who have nursed him so oft, best know this.)

my Bowels fm—

Was he not perpetually in debt, borrowing of us often, and never making recompense: full of ambitious schemes, but in~~comparable~~ capable of the ~~mod~~ most modest exertions?

Is he not the most negligent of fathers & husbands? And most unfortunately prey to _infatuation_?"
I had to admit, all this was true.

"Well then—" continued William, "perhaps you will concede, that his coming to stay with us, had always a most disruptive effect upon our work & the harmonious courses of our lives"
I granted this, in part.

—"Is not that a falcon?" remarked Wm, by the bye, gazing like an eagle into the sun.
I could not but agree.

"As to Cholericke, the rift is not entirely without benefits, my dear. Do you recall, the deep joy & tranquillity of our retired life together—just you & I?"

"Oh _yes_, William!"

Alas, Alas, Alas! I am justly punished, for my presumption in glancing into your journal, dear Dorothy! 'Tis all too true! At the thought of my inadequacies would to Heaven it were not! O dear dear Dorothy!

He squeezed my hand — my heart leapt.

"Would not we both benefit, from a restoration of that tranquillity? I know my work would. It has suffered greatly through Chollericke's caprices"

"Oh has it dear William? How terrible!"

"Can you not imagine my dear sister, the balm it would be to my bosom, to repose in your company and yours alone? I at my work, you at your sweet domestic tasks — Dinner in the orchard, or tea beneath the portugal-laurel … Evenings by the fireside — I shall read Paradise Lost to you, & you may rest your head on my knee."

He patted my head affectionately.

"I think it will be little short of Heav'n, Dorothy," he concluded — at which my whole being seemed to thrill with ecstasy.

August 12th — There followed here some 2 weeks of Scottish touring, which passed for me in a haze of happiness. Alone with my Beloved! (Except of course

So, the TAROT was right!

that he spent whole days in solitary mountain walking.) How eagerly I have made arrangements at each
inn, for his especial comfort! How gladly I wrestled,
with sour & slatternly landladies, for a supper.

With what triumph did I, one evening, preside over
a whole young salmon, boyled!

"It is a pity," observed William, "that they have
neglected the cucumber. But of course, if we were at
home, my dear — I know that no delicious detail
would be spared —"

And he smiled a smile of such deep happiness.
my heart almost burst.

I wonder how the scarlet beans are doing? And
how Iris is managing? ~~And if poor Cholericke~~

August 13th

Today Wm abruptly abandoned his plan, to walk
over the Rummock's O'Scatterpee and suddenly said,
"Let us return home, Dorothy."
With what rapture, did I hear these sweet words!

GORSEMERE

Remorse
Ogres
Ogee
Mere
Seem
Seemer
Rose
Gore
Sore
Some
~~Gome~~
Sere
Sego
(I think it should)
be 'a'
Rome
Merge
Serge

I am bitten all over from the dismally infested beds, have not changed my linen, for 6 weeks; or washed my head; but of course, as long as my darling was contented, these discomforts were as nothing.

Today we set forth from MacSlithery, to dear Gorsmere! How I long for its familiar beauty!

September 1st

I have not written in my journal for many days. It has rained incessantly since we left MacSlithery, I am soaked to the very sprockets of my stays. I do hope my darling will not catch cold.

We are tonight lodged at the Toad and Earwig, so tomorrow should bring us to dear Gorsemere at last.

September 2nd

The longed-for day dawned: and a beautiful day, with a perfect mild rain, that made my heart leap up. As we rode once more upon the dear stones of Ambleside, Wm seized my hand and kissed it.

Here we abandoned the cart, determined to walk the last few miles to our beloved home. An evening of sweet grey mist, the dear familiar Pratincole calling among the boulders.

As we turned into our own lovely vale, & saw the smokes of Gorsemere rising straight up like blue threads to heaven, I laid my head on William's shoulder and felt as if I were entering Paradise.

From henceforth our lives would be bathed in the most exquisite tranquillity: no riotous guests to disturb our felicity, no intoxications to blind our sight: only work, peace & quiet, & each other's beloved company. My heart near burst for quiet joy.

We saw, among the trees, our own roof gleam in the gentle rain; we smelt the honeysuckle, the scarlet beans, grown very tall, nodded to us as we passed up the path, flung open the door, & beheld—

—Good heavens!—————

CHOLERICKE!

Nostrils wrong again

He leapt up & fell upon William's bosom. —"Oh my dear William!" he cried. "Forgive me! Best of men, most towering of poetic genii—embrace me once more as a brother! Let me kiss your noble feet, adorned with the mud of your own Northern roads! Colossus among men! Say you forgive!"

"Would you put on the kettle, please, Dorothy?" requested William.

I hastened to the kitchen, where I found Iris very bonny, pickling some thistles. She said Cholericke had arrived yesterday & slept some 15 hours, but seemed v. sober. As I busied myself about the tea, the shock of Cholericke's arrival dissolv'd into a great joy, that the estrangement between us was mended.

We will encourage our dear friend in ways of prudence and sobriety. In his penitential mood, what might he not achieve? His Reading is Enormous, I know.

So: our lives can still, I am sure, be bathed in exquisite tranquillity: work, peace and quiet,

Reading
DLABACŽ
FÜSSLI
PÖPPELMAN
POZZO
STURM
PRETZEL
RÖD-HEISS
PAUKER
HARPIK
PARTIJ-
PUPER
SNOTBALS
FISSCHERN-
ZJIPS
NOZTRILZ
TOHNAILSS
ANBUMPZA-
DAIZEE

We will study Baroque Art!

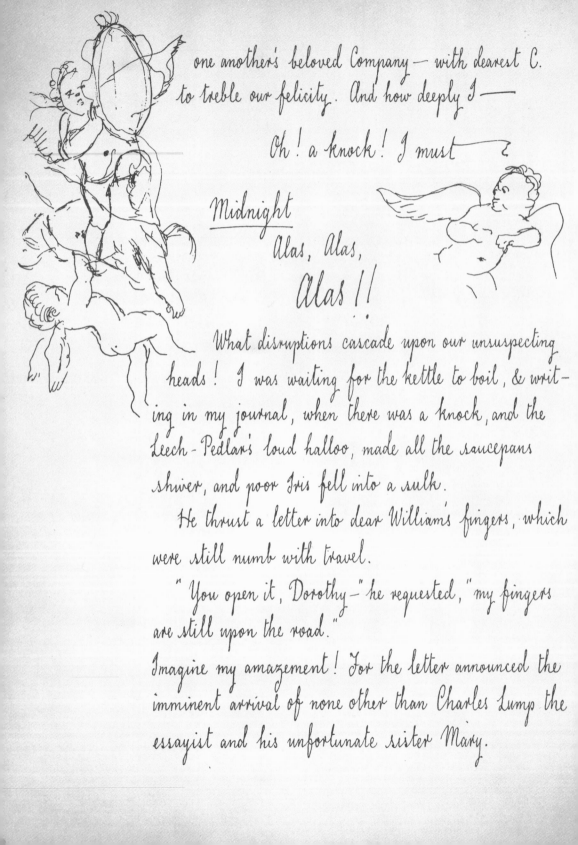

one another's beloved Company — with dearest C.
to treble our felicity. And how deeply I —

Oh! a knock! I must

Midnight

Alas, Alas,

Alas!!

What disruptions cascade upon our unsuspecting
heads! I was waiting for the kettle to boil, & writing in my journal, when there was a knock, and the
Leech-Pedlar's loud halloo, made all the saucepans
shiver, and poor Iris fell into a sulk.

He thrust a letter into dear William's fingers, which
were still numb with travel.

"You open it, Dorothy—" he requested, "my fingers
are still upon the road."

Imagine my amazement! For the letter announced the
imminent arrival of none other than Charles Lump the
essayist and his unfortunate sister Mary.

"Good G——!" I cried in alarm, "When are they expected?" "In about half a minute, I should say, Milady," replied the Leech-Pedlar, "they're a-loiterin' by the wash house wall."

"Tell them to come in!" I cried, tho' my heart beat like a wild peewit's, when her nest is threatened, by a herd of bullocks — for I knew only too well the sad case of Mrs Lump.

"Tell 'em yoursen!" cried the Leech Pedlar, "I ain't a-speakin' to yon lady — 'tis plain as a pillock, ye can see by th'rollin' of her eye, that her's been queered by th' Evil One!"

And crossing himself, he made his escape, up the chimney.

"Silly fellow!" cried Cholericke, "away with your superstitions! 'Tis only a madness, my dear Dorothy — and fitful only — at times Miss Lump is quite lucid — 'tis only when her fit is on her that she is stark mad, & even then, the gibbering is the worst of it. I shall conduct them indoors —"

"All the same, hide the knives & forks, Dorothy,"

O. Bloody Hellebore (Helleborus Sanguineus) with a decoction of which, Gerard says, Dioscorides wrote that Melampos purged his mad daughter's melancholy.

commanded William, "I seem to recall, that Miss Lumps had the misfortune, to stab her aged mother, thro' the heart, in one of her fits!"

I seized the cutlery, and thrust them down my <u>stays</u> — only just in time, for the door opened, and Cholericke presented to us his old friends.

They were both small, dark & fatigued. Mr Lump very civil, his sister quiet. Though she had a fat <u>thrush</u>* upon her bonnet, I thought it best not to comment upon it!

THRUSH — *Actually Singing

The Lumps

W^m inspired by the moment, jotted down this

C. says the head is too thick.

THRUSH

From this fair face had Reason fled
We saw at once, 'twas ~~clear~~ plain
And yet a Thrush sat on her head
Singing thro' hail and rain.
It sang as if its heart would burst
O happy creature, she
I ~~did~~ could not think her madness curst
No more than bird-thronged tree.

W.W.

(Inspired! My dear journal honoured as a vessel for his outpourings!)

Well —

I made them as welcome as I could, tho' every time I moved, I rattled, with the hidden knives & forks, & as I bent down to offer Miss Lump a cup of tea, I was seized with such a stabbing pain, I was afraid I was about to despatch myself, myself (as it were). I excused myself, went to arrange tea — moved as carefully as possible, to the scullery door, but alas! I was about to withdraw, when a great cascade of knives & forks fell from the secret recesses of my person, and bounced insolently upon the flagstones.

"Good heavens!" I cried, tho' my poor imagination seemed quite starved of inspiration, for an excuse— "I wondered, where Iris had put the knives & forks!" & fled, red-faced, to the scullery.

I set about supper, tho' Iris, not expecting our return until St. Vera's Day (Sept 12ᵗʰ) had almost nothing in the pantry. However, at this moment, we heard the hoarse, barking KWOWK of the Short-Eared Owl. Iris darted into the garden, & fell upon the creature, which was feasting upon a field-vole by the Necessary.

Iris despatched it, pluck'd it, & stuffing it with the reliques of the field-vole, put it to roast in pigs lard.

"Aha!" said William, looking in to the scullery during these preparations, "I see you are preparing a Black Winged Stilt, for the pot."

Thank G——, Iris held her tongue. (Wᵐ is not correctible on these matters.)

Owl & Vole
or
Intimations
of Mortality

Iris's
cure against
the Phrensie:

Take leaves &
floures of
Primrose,
boil them in
a little Fountaine
Water, & in some
rose & Betony
waters, add sugar,
pepper, salt &
butter, roll 'em
into small balls
& thrust them
into the patients
ears.

Primrose
Balls

A strange sound of struggle from the parlour, inter-
rupted our preparations: William and I rushed in to
find Miss Lump, tearing down the curtains, with every
appearance of frenzy: Cholericke and Mr Lump sat
tranquilly by the fire, discussing Measure for Measure.

"It is best to ignore it," whispered Mr Lump, in an
aside.

"Besides" cried Cholericke, "what are curtains? What
do we want with such bourgeois contraptions?"
I must admit I felt a grievous pang at the damage
to the curtains: I had contrived them from a pair of
William's nether-garments, when we first came to
Vole Cottage. I withdrew to the kitchen to recover
my composure.

But no sooner had I sat down upon the stool
by the range, than the oven door burst open, & to my
utter astonishment, the owl flew out, quite bald, &
glistening, & flapped round the room, expelling bits
of vole with great violence, as it went.

"They be marvellous tough creeturs, Missus,"

Iris explained, chasing it with a broom-handle — but I could not help thinking its miraculous recovery must be due in some measure to the carelessness of Iris's preparations.

The owl swept all the saucepans from their hooks, & they crashed down with ear-splitting cacophony upon the flagstones: Iris, striking at it with the broom, had the misfortune to dislodge the old clock, which keeled over sideways & struck me upon the head. I was so stunned, as to see shooting-stars for several minutes: through which galaxy William's dear face materialised, like the visage of the Almighty peeping thro' the Firmament.

"I trust this is not an inconvenient moment for a private word, Dorothy," he murmured, tho' I could scarce hear his words for the striking of the clock, which struck continuously from that moment & is striking still. I struggled to give my Darling the attention he deserved, tho' my head still rang, and the owl flying up & down, and Iris chasing it, were distracting enough,

True Love Knot
(Paris Quadrifolia)

I fear.

"I will not beat about the bush, Dorothy," said William, seizing my hand, and gazing at me with such unexpected warmth, it threw me into a lather.

"I must confess it, my dear sister," he continued, "I can contain it no longer! Above all persons alive I love and value you, my dear sister—"

My heart bounded, at his words, quite thro' my stays.

"And believe me, I would not hurt you for the world," he smiled. At this moment the owl whizzed past his nose, but he appeared not to notice it. "My dear sister" he continued, "you will, I am sure, rejoice to hear that I am engaged to be married!"

At this news, the world went dark, and I felt myself reeling on the edge of an abyss—I clutched the chopping board, & screamed aloud—

Henbane

"Your joy is understandable, my dear," said William, helping me to a chair, "and your delight will increase a hundredfold when I tell you the identity of my Bride to be—

awaiting his return to consciousness, my breast *a perfect*

background of wild & whirling thoughts; I can only confide my

tis none other than dear <u>Mary</u>!" (O Wonder!)

At that moment Iris, aiming at the Owl perched on the
mantel, unluckily brought the broom down upon dear
William's skull — & he fell insensible, to the floor.

With Cholericke's help, we got him upstairs & to bed, tho'
I could not forbear <u>screaming</u> <u>aloud</u> every step of the way,
at the blows which fortune is <u>raining</u> upon us. —

— Miss Lump, rampant downstairs upon the pianoforte
(I can hear her <u>running up & down the keys</u>) —

— Our guest's supper flying around the kitchen, leaving
<u>chaos</u> in its wake —

— My dearest William struck insensible — his organ
of Poetic Discourse perhaps <u>gone for ever</u> !! =

— and above all! <u>This Dreadful Wedding</u> !!!
O How can it be? After his many speeches about the
Sweet Solitude he enjoys with <u>me</u>? And who has lured
him from my side? Can it (O heav'n!) be Mary
Godwit, for whom he showed such a marked approval?
(But she is already married — or does that not matter,
these days?) or could it be (O <u>Heav'n</u> & <u>Earth</u>!)
poor <u>Mary Lump</u> ??? Can it be that dear

(left margin) I sit by his bedside. He stirs! I cannot — betray me!! ... pursued a courtship to the verge of engagement, without <u>deceiving</u> me ? ... at the last. ... my dear journal, Alas, Alas! Even my dear journal ... This is the last page & I have no other Book, for C. is Beyond Rational Intercourse again, but

(bottom margin) interest in anything has gone that far ??? How can he have

(right margin) Williams